Lions
of the
Sea

Printed in Victoria, Canada

Though based on a true incident, this is a work of fiction. All characters-even those based on real people-are entirely fictional.

Summary: A fictionalized journal relates the experiences aboard the Komagata Maru.

A cataloguing record for this book that includes the U.S. Library of Congress Classification number, the Library of Congress Call number and the Dewey Decimal cataloguing code is available from the National Library of Canada. The complete cataloguing record can be obtained from the National Library's online database at: www.nlc-bnc.ca/amicus/index-e.html

TRAFFORD

This book was published *on-demand* in cooperation with Trafford Publishing.
On-demand publishing is a unique process and service of making a book available for retail sale to the public taking advantage of on-demand manufacturing and Internet marketing.
On-demand publishing includes promotions, retail sales, manufacturing, order fulfilment, accounting and collecting royalties on behalf of the author.

Suite 6E, 2333 Government St., Victoria, B.C. V8T 4P4, CANADA

Phone	250-383-6864	Toll-free	1-888-232-4444 (Canada & US)
Fax	250-383-6804	E-mail	sales@trafford.com
Web site	www.trafford.com	TRAFFORD PUBLISHING IS A DIVISION OF TRAFFORD HOLDINGS LTD.
Trafford Catalogue #03-1679		www.trafford.com/robots/03-1679.html	

10   9   8   7   6   5   4   3

Dedicated to the memory of the passengers
of the
Komagata Maru

Prologue

A full moon shone above while a fierce wind dragged swollen clouds across the sky. One minute there was light, and the next, impenetrable darkness. The air was thick with smoke and the stinging smell of slaughtered humanity. The young turbaned police sergeant smelled the heavy air and listened to the moans and shrieks of wounded men scattered across the grassy plain before him. Watching the sky, he marched through the brush and felt the crunch of dry grass under his feet. He stopped suddenly, sensing something wet and muddy. His heart pounded heavily. His eyes dropped slowly. He had stepped in a pool of blood. He examined the dark pool, then dragged his eyes across the yellow grass to the body of a man hidden in the shadows. The man was thin and gaunt. He wore a dark turban and a strong beard. His hands were rough and calloused, and they covered and pressed against a fresh wound in his stomach. The blood filled his hands, poured through his fingers, streamed down his jacket, and emptied into the darkness. The sergeant's eyes slipped over the cotton pants, the three-button European style jacket, and the shining iron kara. At last his gaze found the man's face where two dark eyes reflected an incandescent moon and made two gleaming pearls.

The British troops trudged along the railway tracks, searched the ditch, and made sure no hiding place had been overlooked. The sergeant squatted beside the body and watched the glowing pearls turn into beads. He leaned forward and extended his arm to shut the eyes. As his fingers approached the face, the beads turned back to pearls and the eyes blazed with sudden life. The man grabbed the sergeant's wrist and pulled him closer with startling force. The man wheezed and coughed and struggled with unintelligible words. Then, reaching into his jacket, he revealed a journal and placed it in the sergeant's hand. "My son!" he said, "Give it to my son!" He released the sergeant's wrist, sighed his last breath, and the pearls were beads again.

The next morning a writer would dispassionately report that a group of treasonous Hindu seditionists had come to agitate the good people of India in a desperate attempt to ignite the fires of revolution and cause civil unrest. The next morning the writer would hide the truth under a mountain of lies and half-truths. But had the writer weighed the story on all scales, seen the story in other lights, perhaps even possessed a different set of eyes; strong and discerning eyes, deeper and darker eyes, eyes free and able to see beyond the distorted peephole of his master, then perhaps that very same writer would have written a slightly different story. Yes, had the writer served those who lived history rather than those who made, moulded, and disguised history, perhaps that writer would have written an entirely different story. A story about fathers. A story about Sikh and Hindu and Muslim fathers who would cross rugged mountains, swim endless seas, and face any foe just to put a scrap of food in their baby's stomach. The sergeant opened the journal and read such a story.

MAY 1914

May 1

My son, my dear son, every time I close my eyes I think about you. Now, in the darkness that envelops me, I see you. You are my light: you're playing games in the field behind our home, chasing monsters and creatures and all sorts of apparitions only you can see; you're teasing your mother, constantly following her through the village, repeating her every word like a pesky little parrot; you're chasing lizards around the yard, trying your very best to evade your morning bath; and now I can see you sleeping in your mother's arms, your beautiful mother's arms, much too scared to sleep alone. What were you afraid of? Are you still afraid? I was once afraid like you and, like you, I slept in my mother's arms. Never once did I admit this to anyone; but now, to you, I confess: I was afraid. Of what? I still don't know. Some nameless beast that, if it did exist, existed only in the dark recesses of my mind; but I suppose, for a child, what lives and breathes in the imagination is more real than anything seen or felt or touched by grown-ups.

And now I am afraid. I am more afraid than I have ever been in my life. Afraid of this forced separation that already feels like forever! I wish I didn't have to leave, but our land is barren; nothing grows, and whatever does struggle out of our desolate soil is stolen from our plates and given to some faraway King who already has too much to eat. Your mother doesn't eat so that you may eat, and I cannot sleep because I cannot provide. There is nothing left in Punjab for the farmer, and this farmer must take his chances elsewhere within the Empire.

7

I suppose, at least, there lies one benefit of being a subject: I can search for new land to work on so long as it belongs to the King. I have heard of many and much better opportunities in Europe and Asia, but these are all foreign places and I cannot take even the slightest chance with my family's future; I can afford only one fare and must go to a place where there is no chance of being turned back. Canada is a golden place full of promise and hope for any hardworking subject of the Empire. I've heard many rumours from soldiers who have already been there and who have had nothing but good things to say about the land and the people. One soldier even read to the entire village an article from some British newspaper that glorified the Sikh soldier: his strength, his courage, his loyalty in battle. And not too long ago a villager, who reads and understands English, read a leaflet that was practically begging for farmers from all over Europe to move to Canada to take care of unused, lush, fertile land. There's more good and generous land in Canada than there are people to take care of it; so much that they give it to foreigners! Foreigners who never paid the tax we paid; foreigners who never sent fathers and brothers to war to protect, strengthen, and expand the Empire. I can't even begin to imagine how they'll treat a strong Punjabi farmer like me; a man who went hungry to pay their abhorrent taxes, a man who is less because of the friends and family he lost in distant lands to expand and protect the Empire. Canada wants farmers? They will have no greater farmer! No more missed meals, son. No more tears in the night for a stomach so empty it screams and pounds and refuses to let you drift into forgetful dreams. You and your mother will live in a world of abundance. Abundance! And that, my son, is a promise.

But still there is regret. The regret for leaving you is agonizing. It weighs heavily on my soul. You cannot even begin to imagine--and will not be able to until you yourself are a father--the anguish, the deep and profound anguish of the father who by no fault of his own cannot provide for his family. Even now my heart bleeds when I think of the day I left you. That horrible day will forever be the worst day of my life. Never should a father be separated from his family. Never.

Now, whenever I see a father playing with his child, tears fill my eyes, a mist of despair quickly spreads over me, and I can no longer speak or even think straight for the shame is unbearable. That you refused to say good-bye to your own father is understandable; you are barely five-years-old. And though I understand your anger and deep disappointment, I only wished you were old enough to hear the pain and quivering hesitation in my voice as I tried my very best to win your attention and gain your approval. Then you would have said good-bye. I know it. And though you couldn't hear the anguish in my voice, your mother did, as she is, and always will be, a master of my thousand and one tones. It is because of your mother's divine wisdom that I take you with me, for just as I was leaving she handed me this journal and said, "So he will know." And so, my son, my dear beloved son, with this journal I take you with me, and one day, when you are old enough, you will know. You will know that I sacrificed our precious time together, not to escape responsibility, but to bring you every opportunity a father could ever wish upon his son.

Now I'm in Japan. I'm in an alley near a dock beside a man named Sunny, who, like me, awaits to board the Komagata Maru in the morning. He's a short man with chubby cheeks and a most terrible habit of talking to himself. Often I think he's talking to me, but, when I ask him to repeat himself, he shakes his head and claims he wasn't talking to me. I look around to see who he was talking to and figure he probably sees and hears things I cannot see or hear. His turban is tied sloppily and he wears an oversized, travel-wrinkled European suit, which he practically floats in. It was probably handed down from a thicker and taller older brother. He has thick, bristly eyebrows that connect at the ridge of his nose and a wild, black, bushy beard he has probably never attempted to groom or tame in his life. Now he is nervous because he doesn't have the fare for passage. But he feels that he might be able to persuade Gurdit Singh, the charterer, to let him board nevertheless. As I write this, he is going through his words, rehearsing his arguments, and doing a pretty decent job at convincing an old busted barrel that when he reaches the Dominion of Canada he will work from dawn to dusk and dawn again just to pay the fare, plus interest.

I've heard many things about Gurdit Singh, and one of those things is that he is a shrewd businessman. I have known many shrewd businessmen in my life and none of them were gift-givers. Sunny will ask for free passage and Gurdit will laugh and argue that if he made an

9

exception this time, and the other passengers found out, then everyone would want the same favour and he would no longer be a shrewd businessman but a warm philanthropist. Then he would assure him that there was no profit in philanthropy, and that no philanthropist could successfully charter and provision a ship like the Komagata Maru across an expanse as immense as the Pacific. If I could help Sunny, I would; but I hardly make the fare myself, and to fund this journey we've had to mortgage our home and land and borrow money from our kind and most generous neighbours. But not in vain; it will take me about a year or so to settle in Canada and, just as soon as I do, you and your mother will join me, and together we will work hard to save money and bring our neighbours down.

May 2

Before dawn Sunny and I stood before the Komagata Maru waiting to board. As the sun rose and illuminated the steamer with its golden rays, we took one look at him and then turned to each other with wide eyes. We were both dismayed by its degraded presence. The ancient ship creaked and moaned and complained over a breathing sea. He was so rusted and out of repair that I wondered how he could possibly remain afloat. He was approximately three hundred feet long and thirty feet wide and was covered with flaking, chipping, and peeling paint. We gazed at each other again, breathlessly; then we instinctively searched the ship for passengers, desperately hoping that he wasn't ours. But, soon enough, we heard voices and we saw turbans moving about. All was confirmed. Sunny gasped and muttered, "Waheguru," and made his way for the gangplank. I shook my head with disbelief and thought that, if I didn't have you and your mother back home, I'd probably turn and run as far away as I could from this hideous hunk of rusted metal. I muttered, "Waheguru," and followed Sunny.

I was both right and wrong about Gurdit: he is both a shrewd businessman and a warm philanthropist. When we walked across the gangplank and set our first steps upon the crippled steamer, Gurdit, an older man with a tightly wound white turban and a perfectly groomed

10

white beard, greeted us with a benign smile. Sunny immediately bowed, touched his feet, rose quickly, and, quivering with nervousness, said, "Babaji, I have heard so many good things about you. I have heard so many good things about you, Babaji. You are a great and strong leader, Babaji, and you make our ancestors proud. You make our people proud and give poor farmers a chance to make something good with themselves..." At this point Gurdit read the desperation in his face and understood. He began to shake his head slowly, but before he could refuse him or say anything, Sunny continued: "I can do anything, Babaji. I can do anything. I can clean, cook, I can scrub, I can scrub so good we could eat our meals off the floor." Gurdit lifted his chin, narrowed his gaze and, in a stern voice, said, "What's the problem here?" Sunny answered, "Please, Babaji, please, I will keep the ship spotless." Gurdit looked around the ship; it was already spotless. He laughed and said, "Do not worry. We shall all share in the duties." Sunny continued, "Please, Babaji, my wife is pregnant and my son is sick and I have no money." Gurdit sighed, put his hand on Sunny's shoulder, and said, "Brother, everyone here shares your story." Sunny dropped his head; he said, "Please...no one will know..."

There was a long silence. Gurdit looked Sunny up and down; then he indicated me and said, "He will know." I lowered my head and swore I had heard nothing. Gurdit laughed at my words and, after a moment, he said firmly, "I cannot. I cannot make an exception. Suppose you told someone and then that someone told someone...then, the next thing you know, the whole ship discovered you didn't pay. Then everyone would demand their money back, and when I couldn't give it to them for having spent it all on provisions, why, they'd make me walk the plank!" Gurdit paused, combed his beard with his fingers, and let his eyes evaluate Sunny. After a reflective moment, he sighed a sigh of personal defeat and said, "But I tell you what...suppose you snuck on." Sunny lifted his eyes, shocked. "Suppose I turned around," continued Gurdit, "to stare at them seagulls over there, and you snuck on. Then you're a stowaway, and if you go around opening your mouth about what you did, then it will be you who walks the plank and not me." Sunny gazed at him with wet, grateful eyes, and Gurdit turned to stare at some faraway seagulls. Sunny whispered his thanks, took his bags, and boarded. When Sunny was gone,

11

Gurdit turned to me and asked, "Did you see anything?" I shook my head dumbly. He smiled a majestic smile and said, "Neither did I."

I paid Gurdit one hundred dollars to board and he gave me a brief, yet informative, tour. Though the ship was clean, it hardly seemed seaworthy, and, when I asked about the ship's overall integrity, he said it was the best of the three steamers he could afford, and that the other two ships were a lot cheaper but would have capsized a mile into the journey. He then laughed heartily and said that at least this one would make it half-way, so long as we didn't meet up with any whales, which I didn't find very funny. Then he said that he and the passengers had renamed the ship Nanak Jahaz, which somewhat reassured me. Nanak Jahaz, he assured me, would take care of us.

Nanak Jahaz is a fairly large steamer with a small Japanese crew. They seem capable and competent and cheery; they carry a sure and positive attitude, and so I feel I have little, if anything, to worry about. There is much to be said about attitude, and there is something about Gurdit's attitude that makes me feel comfortable. I have always found it both strange and remarkable how a person's demeanour can inspire confidence or anxiety in others.

Gurdit led me to the lower deck where he and a few other men-- men who form the passengers committee--had spent days upon days preparing for the voyage while anchored in Hong Kong. The steamer was mostly used to transport coal, so you can imagine how filthy it must have been and how long it must have taken to clear it out, scrub and lime wash the floor, and then to install and bolt to the floor what I gather to be approximately two or three hundred backless benches and a dozen or so latrines. There is also a small communal kitchen that everyone can use to prepare their meals, though some men have been designated as cooks. Gurdit, an intelligent man, went on to explain how it was imperative that we all work together to keep the ship clean and organized for our comfort, safety, and hygiene. "This," he said in his firm and commanding voice, "will be a journey with men unaccustomed to sea travel, men unaccustomed to being separated from their families, so no effort must be spared to keep spirits high and strong." I agreed. He showed me to my bunk and then returned to the upper deck to take care of some business. Having on Nanak Jahaz far more stowaways than he had anticipated, he needed to take on a shipment of coal in order to pay the last instalment of the charter. Apparently, he has a buyer in Vancouver.

When the coal was loaded, the passengers assembled on deck. Under a bright and clear sky, a shrill whistle blew; and we said good-bye to the trees, the docks, the boats, the land. Then suddenly, a young boy, about five or six years of age, began to sing a hymn. It wasn't long before everyone joined in, and we were singing our fears and anxieties out of our hearts. With Waheguru's name on our lips, we welcomed the sea, the journey, and the uncertainty to come.

When the land disappeared and all that surrounded us were two deserts of blue, the men melted away and returned to their bunks. I leaned on the rail and stared at the horizon, and the horizon didn't seem to get any closer or further; it didn't seem to move at all. Sunny grabbed the rail beside me, watched the horizon a short moment, then turned to me and looked into my eyes as though he had something deep and serious to say. He tilted his head and asked, "What does it mean, 'walk the plank'?" I laughed and explained what I knew of the expression. He pretended to listen and understand, nodding his head periodically, carefully following my lips, but not really listening.

It wasn't long before he expressed his thoughts. He looked up to the heavens, breathed the fresh sea air and said, "My boy will have land." He laughed, screamed his excitement, and continued, "Yes! He will have acres of good, good, fat and juicy, lush and giving land, land so generous he will eat like the King himself! And he will never have to let his son go to bed without a good, fat fill." He paused, closed his eyes, and then, opening his eyes with a start, said, "My boy will go to school. He will learn English and he will know the books like English gentlemen." He turned to me, and an uncontrollable joy filled his eyes. He threw his gaze and arms to the sky and yelled, "Waaaaheeeguru!" His body turned rigid with hope and happiness and all around men stared at us with large, understanding smiles. Then he grabbed me and twirled me and yelled over and over again, "My boy will have land!" And I understood every ounce of happiness within his soul, for I felt the same happiness, the same joy: the joy of a father given a second chance.

May 3

Nanak Jahaz ploughs through a troubled sea and the latrines are a mess.
Those plagued with seasickness, who are many and uncounted, stay on
deck near the rail, ready to deposit their mess over the side. It's not
uncommon to see a man pale and green suddenly dash for a latrine or the
upper deck. As for myself, I am fine, and, thankfully, so are my neighbours.

I have a tall and lanky ex-soldier named Amar for a neighbour. He
wears an old worn khaki uniform and he is quiet. His eyes are the cold
and dead, expressionless as a snake. He spends his time staring vacantly
at Sunny, who has already expressed some concern to me. He despises
the way Amar looks at him. Whenever Sunny begins to tell one of his tall
tales, as he's predisposed to do as his father was once a great storyteller,
Amar just stares at him and, somehow, that abominable gaze penetrates
Sunny to the point where he must turn his back on Amar so as to be able
to continue his tale comfortably and without distraction. It's as if Amar
can't stand anyone showing even the slightest measure of happiness, so
he, knowingly or unknowingly, steals it from others and spreads his
gloom everywhere.

There are also the two middle aged men who act like children and
look like brothers. Ali and Sanjay, both clean-shaven and both in
European suits, are constantly competing with each other. Just a moment
ago, Sanjay nearly killed himself in a most ridiculous attempt to prove a
point. Sunny had just finished telling us a story about a man who could
hold his breath for over five minutes when Sanjay, lying under a thin,
wool blanket, and holding his potbelly, blurted, "I could do that." Ali
snorted and said that Sanjay couldn't hold his breath for longer than a
minute. To which Sanjay challenged, "Bet I could hold it longer than
you!" And so it began. Ali said, as if it were a game they often played,
"Winner gets his clothes washed for two days." Now sitting up, Sanjay
replied, "Make it three!" Ali laughed at his confidence. He said, "Prepare
to prune those baby hands!" Soon Sunny and I were involved. I had to
count to three at which point they would hold their breaths. Then I would
put my hand in front of Ali's mouth and Sunny would put his hand in
front of Sanjay's mouth, and we would signal the end of the competition

14

when a breath was released and consequently taken. I counted to three, they swallowed a deep breath and held it in. No sooner did they begin than Ali gave up, but Sanjay held on strong. He turned blue as the sky, then purple as a grape, and even when we pleaded with him to breathe, assuring him that he had won, he stubbornly refused, and only released his breath when he fell unconscious. When he regained consciousness, Ali, a sore loser, said that his friend had hardly held his breath a minute and that he shouldn't have to do his laundry. Though, really, it probably was five minutes! None of us have the luxury of a clock.

May 4

Fewer passengers are sick, and most of us are trying to keep the ship clean. Ali spent the whole day washing clothes in a leaky bucket while Sanjay towered over him, criticizing the way he washed clothes, telling him how his mother used to clean his clothes, how his wife cleaned his clothes, and how he wished his clothes to be cleaned. Twice Ali nearly kicked the bucket over, and more than a dozen times threatened to throw his clothes overboard.

In the afternoon I toured the ship with Sunny, and if one thing is certain, those who organized this voyage deserve their own quarters above; besides, two of them have their families with them. I have no complaints nor does anyone below.

Sunny and I marvelled at the feat Gurdit had accomplished and our questions were numerous. First of all, we wondered, how would one go about finding a ship? Does one just walk around the docks shopping and haggling like one does at a bazaar? Or is it a far more complicated affair? And once one finds a ship, how does one judge its seaworthiness? Gurdit had mentioned that this ship was chosen among two other ships that would have surely capsized. How did he know that? And how does he know for certain that this ship won't! Maybe he has a knack for ships as he does for people. In any case, all ships look the same to me, one iron monster indistinguishable from the next. I wouldn't have been able to pick one; but, then again, I can't even tell a bad mango from a good one.

I always left those decisions to your beloved mother. I dearly miss her, and you.

May 5

The breathing sea is in my ears, in my bones, in my thoughts, and Nanak Jahaz creaks and groans and sighs as we plough through the night, making slow but steady progress toward Canada. Everyone grows stronger and stronger. It is the nature of man to either adapt to his situation or be defeated by it, and it is not the nature of this ship to be so easily defeated. Now some of us walk the ship like high and mighty sailors ready to conquer all the weather may throw our way. And if this voyage is working so smoothly, if everyone is working so well together, it is because Gurdit is a fair and organized leader who understands people: their dreams, their hopes, their ambitions, and their fears. But most of all, he is a father, and he understands the father's need to be the best father he can be, for he has a boy, a boy who runs around the ship, always singing and playing and leading two other boys into all kinds of trouble. His boy is his spitting image. And it is hard for me to look at those three boys and not think of you. I miss you and your mother; so much that I keep myself busy cleaning things that don't need to be cleaned, fixing things that don't need to be fixed, doing all kinds of absurd and menial tasks in a desperate attempt to prevent memories from depressing my spirit and sinking me into a dark and depthless ocean of despair. I miss home.

In the evening, when Sunny senses my despair, he turns his back on Amar and goes out of his way to tell me a tale that is sure to make me laugh, and, no sooner does he begin than Ali and Sanjay gather to listen. He has a knack for storytelling, and a talent for lifting a man's spirit. If ever I were to attend university in England like my cousin, I would write my thesis on friendship! How friends are made, how they are maintained, and how they are the heart's lifeboat in that dark and depthless ocean. In any case, Sunny is a man alive with stories, expressions, and antidotes, and it took a while, but most of us are now officially accustomed to his inner need to converse with himself aloud; so now when Sanjay or Ali hear him mumbling about, they check to see if he is in fact talking to them, or himself, before they ask him to repeat his words.

16

Last night was calm and peaceful, yet hardly a soul could sleep. The entire ship was alive and electric with the whispered hopes and dreams of men far too eager and excited for the days to come; men who were much too afraid to lose even a second of what was, for them, the first few moments of an answered prayer. For the passengers knew that time would begin from the moment they set foot in Canada, and that they would discuss their journey, from raising the money for the fare, to leaving their loved ones, to reaching Canada, and, finally, to sending their family their savings so that they could once again be reunited. Then they imagined their family's first steps on Canadian soil, and how they would need to teach them about everything they had learned about life in Canada. And finally, they imagined recounting their harrowing journey, over and over again, as their fathers had done to them and their grandfathers had done to their fathers, each time, of course, exaggerating their story a slight degree more than the last, so that the final version transformed into a tale utterly foreign to the original, though definitely more inspiring and entertaining.

My father had such a story, which he first told me when he realized I could understand Punjabi. It started off as:

"A long time ago when I had only one shirt and one pair of pants, I came upon a lost elephant trudging toward our neighbouring village. So, unafraid of the beast, I stood before it and touched its soft trunk and slowly led it back into the forest."

It was a nice story about an encounter with an elephant, but it didn't leave the impression he had desired. So, as I grew older it turned into:

"A long time ago when I had only one shirt and one pair of pants and no shoes, I came upon an angry elephant moving toward a neighbouring village. The bull growled at me as if a beast possessed, but I didn't shrink away from the threat. I took a step forward and, seeing the strength in my eyes, the bull stopped in its tracks and retreated back to wherever it came from. I thank Waheguru for giving me the strength to face the elephant."

Still not satisfied, when I was old enough to marry he would tell the story like Sunny, with movements and pauses and deep penetrating gazes. He had finally settled on:

"A long, long time ago, when people had it much harder than your generation, when your father was walking everywhere with no shoes. No shoes! You could not even imagine walking around with no shoes. I was walking my normal twenty mile journey to school, with no shoes, wearing my only shirt and my only pair of pants, which I had to wash every day, when I came upon a rogue elephant that was stampeding toward a village; threatening to trample everything in its path. Now, I could have run away to save my shoeless self; yes, I could have, but then I would have been responsible for the death and destruction the great beast had in mind. So, naturally, I had to do something, for this was one of those moments, one of those character defining moments that Waheguru uses to test one's soul. I recognized the moment for what it was and chose to define the moment rather than have the moment define me. I stood before the elephant and, with a mighty scream, held out my hand and commanded it to turn away. The elephant stopped before me and seemed a little puzzled at first. But when it regarded me carefully and saw in my face an unshakeable determination, the coward turned around and retreated to the forest. I thank Waheguru for giving me the opportunity to save a village."

Everyone would marvel him, and only my mother and I would shake our heads and smile with incredible disbelief. I think he settled on this final version only because he couldn't exaggerate the story any more--unless of course he said, "A long time ago when people had it much harder than your generation, when people only grew to be three inches tall and had only three fingers and two toes and fire breathing monsters roamed the country..." I think you understand. Your grandfather had a deep need to exaggerate, exaggerate his past, exaggerate his situation, exaggerate everything. And though the need to exaggerate things may be present in my blood, too, I promise not to exaggerate in here. And, if, at some distant point in the future, when I'm telling the tale of this journey to your children, and suddenly I start to describe sea monsters and water nymphs and my story starts to change drastically from the first time I told it, you will have this journal to remind me of the truth. Or maybe, like I did, you'll allow your poor old father the right to exaggerate.

Before dawn Sanjay woke and gazed at his hands with respect and appreciation. He then shook Ali awake and we all went up on deck for our morning prayers. Ali bowed and said his first prayer of the day with a congregation of twenty or so Muslims while Sunny and I sat with a congregation of Sikhs meditating on Waheguru's name. After our prayers, Sunny and I went below deck to the kitchen where we waited in a line that was slowly progressing toward a table bearing stacks of freshly cooked rotis and cauldrons of daal and aloo and yoghurt. The scent of curry and cumin and coriander rose from the cauldrons and swept through the ship and filled our bodies with a savoury richness so that whoever closed their eyes daydreamed of home. Behind each food station stood a smiling cook serving food in fair and careful portions. Ali and Sanjay, refusing to wait at the end of the line, and seeing me fairly close to the front, acted as if I were a long lost friend. With great enthusiasm, they greeted me and butted in, much to the displeasure of those behind me. But the men didn't do anything; they merely passed a few disapproving comments and left it at that. Eventually, we reached the first cook, who greeted us kindly and ladled daal onto our plates. Sanjay, a great lover of food, any food, pleaded for a bit more aloo, to which the cook shook his head and said he was under strict rules to be cautious with the provisions, as there was just enough food and water to reach Canada. But Sanjay didn't care much for the reason and at every station asked for more food than he had been given and at every station was met with the same response. To my surprise, the last cook recognized Sanjay from the last few days and, with a hearty laugh, shook a disapproving finger at him before he could even open his mouth. When our plates were full, we went up on deck and sat under a brilliant sun and ate our meal in silence. Sanjay, as usual, was the first to finish. The man doesn't eat food, he breathes food. He eats at such speed that I can hardly imagine him enjoying even a single morsel of what enters his mouth. Ali commented laughingly to Sanjay, "Hey, it wouldn't hurt to breathe between bites!" We laughed at the comment. Sanjay looked at Ali, sniffed, and went back to his food.

When our plates were empty, we returned them to the kitchen and helped clean everything up. And it was while washing dishes with Gurdit that I discovered that he was a self-educated man who spoke five languages. He spoke phrases in Mandarin and Malay and French, and then said a few things in English. Of all the languages, I found English to be the dullest. Often in India I've eavesdropped on British authorities speaking their strange language and thought that they may as well be crickets chirping, or cats meowing, or even dogs barking, as every single word sounded the same. At the time I expressed my observations to your mother, and she admonished me, saying that it was a disparaging observation and that the British most likely felt the same about our language. I thought about her words that whole night and soon realized your mother was right--as she often is. It was wrong of me to have thought and said such a thing; to have compared the English language to the sounds of insects and animals. And then it occurred to me: maybe the British had difficulty understanding and appreciating the grace and poetry of Punjabi.

May 7

The day started off clear and blue, but as morning turned into afternoon thunderheads marched across the sky and darkened the world so that everyone stayed below deck for fear of the storm to come. In the evening, Sunny expressed his worry that he wouldn't have enough money for a place to stay in Canada. Ali told him not to worry as he could, without question, stay with him and Sanjay. Amar sighed and shook his head at Sunny's apparent incompetence, and Sunny immediately turned his back on him.

This ex-soldier is making it very difficult for anyone to like him, which is a surprise as every soldier I've ever known has been kind, polite, and helpful. He is none of these. He is expressionless, heartless, and never once have I seen him help maintain the ship; and that amounts to a sin for a group of men who must work together to succeed. All he does is sit below deck, alone, staring at some strange certificate, while everyone else is above scrubbing the decks, cleaning clothes, and enjoying the sun, the sky, and the incredible freshness of the sea air. In the evening, when the sun's warmth begins to abandon the air, we all descend to escape the cold; and when the lower deck begins to fill with cheer, well, Amar drags himself above and stands in the cold by the rail, staring blankly into the darkness, as if he were drawn or moved by it. I suspect he has little idea of or concern for his effect on us; otherwise, I suppose, he wouldn't act as if smiling or caring were an act of mutiny. He may actually believe his attitude is his problem and his problem alone, but when his miserable face influences our day like a dark cloud, it becomes our problem. For his mere presence changes the whole dynamic of our area; and though we try to act as if he didn't exist, we cannot shake his negative effect. Today Sunny called him a walking pin that could burst the bubble on any beautiful day. We all agreed.

Sunny has expressed to me a desire to find a bunk as far away from Amar as possible. But he won't: he has grown far too fond of his audience; and he has grown particularly fond of Ali and Sanjay, who, unbeknownst to them, keep us constantly entertained with their sibling-like squabbles and child-like competitions. As for me, if Sunny moves, I move, for, if Amar is a gloomy cloud that can darken any room, he is counterbalanced by Sunny who is a bright sun, a sun so charged with vitality that he spreads that vitality wherever he wanders. For Sunny has been blessed with true power: the power of influence. And he uses that power not to depress or sink spirits with pessimism or to show all that is dark and evil in the world, but, instead, to enliven with optimism: by searching as best as he can for all that is good in a situation, and by never once failing to enrich, inspire, and entertain us with his stories, with words that constantly remind us of the infinite beauties and riches that lie in every moment.

May 8

The sky and sea and nothing else! I spent the morning gazing at the horizon where two great deserts of blue met and lost themselves in one another. I stared at the clouds and followed one as it journeyed across the sky. As the cloud traversed the sky, it interacted with gusts and sunbeams and other clouds so that its original shape changed in a thousand significant and insignificant ways. I observed the clouds all morning and soon realized that no particular cloud was ever the same at two distinct moments in time.

21

Often, the excited boys stand at the stern and lean toward the water with their eyes fastened to the foam the ship whips as it progresses through the Pacific. They wait patiently for the porpoises that follow Nanak Jahaz and pop their shiny heads out of the deep blue abyss, seeming to bless us with a smile or wink or laugh; and when they do, the boys throw their arms to the sky and cheer, and then talk about the strange creatures all day, refusing to move from the stern even when they are told they must go to sleep.

I can remember when I was a boy and sleep was the enemy and a day held infinite possibilities. How difficult I must have been for my parents who, no matter how hard they tried--and they tried hard--had never been able to keep me in bed. There was no threat great enough to force me to shut my eyes on life, and I always found a way to sneak out of that prison they called my room. If the day held infinite possibilities, the night held infinite mysteries. More than once I snuck out of my room and ran into the darkness and found my tree, which I quickly climbed to watch the stars and fill my soul with Waheguru's grace. Life was so simple then and I rarely understood the problems of grownups. And then I became one. And sleep became a friend. Sleep and dreams held all those possibilities, while the day held only reality, and reality was harsh and unforgiving. It was only when you were born that I realized that the love I had for the infinite possibilities in a day was the same love my parents had for me; for in my eyes they could see what I have always seen in yours: the infinite possibilities of a life. Never in a million years would my father have seen in my eyes a journey across an ocean to live in a land he had only heard about from his superior officers. He smiles down on me now; I know he does, and he knows that his sacrifice was not in vain. I miss him, I miss you. The separation will soon be over.

May 9

A few passengers are seasick again, and the ship's doctor, a short and chubby man, hardly spends time with them. I despise the way he looks at us and the way he won't let his family walk around the ship without his permission. He's constantly giving them commanding looks that silence

22

them instantly, and he never stops ordering them to stay out of the sun. Imagine that! He's a very insecure man, mentally dependent on what white men think of him. Something he learned in the militia no doubt. But his boy always finds a way to escape his tyranny, as boys often do.

I don't think the doctor likes our kind, the farming and labouring kind. Maybe I'm wrong about him, but I'm not the only one who feels this way. If your mother were here she'd know; I'm sure she'd know. She has the intuition of a prophet, whereas I have the intuition of a peanut. But I see it in his eyes. They are the eyes of a master, the eyes of a man who must always be right, even when he knows he is wrong. They are the eyes of a man who loathes his skin colour and wishes he were a degree or two paler, simply because his conquerors convinced him of the superiority of white skin. And he considers himself educated! He seems to look at us and treat us as if we were simple animals, and twice already I've seen him argue with Gurdit in that seemingly passionless language. Over what they were arguing, I don't know. I think Gurdit would like him to spend more time below deck, but that is a place he avoids like a pestilent village. He seems to think he's above the farmer: he's not. He is just a man like all of us, except he has been blessed with the gift of fortune and education. And now Waheguru watches what he does with his blessings, because what he does or does not do with them will determine whether he will deserve future blessings in this life or the next. My father often said that Waheguru gives gifts to those who use them: to those who use their gifts in pursuit of truth and justice, to those who administer rather than to those who horde their luck and fortune from those of lesser fortune; and he used to say, with a most serious face, that Waheguru only spoiled those who could not be spoiled.

The doctor has military experience but he is far from courageous. The fear and insecurity is easy to decipher in his eyes. He fears things we aren't supposed to fear: poverty and death. And he is plagued with the most crippling ailment of all: ego. And so, fearing poverty and death, he is easily manipulated and corrupted. I may not have your mother's intuition, but I do know this: I wouldn't want him in my regiment. As far as I'm concerned he seems to be the type of man who would compromise his entire unit for any slight gain whether that gain is in gold or status. I don't trust him, nobody trusts him, and Sunny constantly makes fun of his arrogant manner. There are even rumours circulating around the ship that he refuses to eat with his hands and that he actually cuts his chapatis with a knife and fork and then uses the fork to dip the chapatis in his daal. How one eats with those silly tools is beyond me; it seems as though the British always find a way to complicate things more than they need to. But it was quite a treat watching Sunny make fun of the doctor, blurting out every now and then the few English phrases he knew, with, of course, a heavy and over exaggerated English accent that drove everyone wild with laughter. When he finished mimicking the doctor, he turned to us with a short tale that immediately made me think of the butt of his imitation, which, I'm sure, was his intention.

"There was once," he began slowly, then waited until we were all paying attention. When we were, he continued, "a beautiful peacock with the most striking feathers you ever saw, which, understandably, made all of the pigeons sick with envy." He paused, gave us a few seconds to imagine beautiful peacocks and jealous pigeons, and then said, "But what the pigeons lacked in beauty they made up for in cleverness and so, through trickery, they convinced one peacock that he was hopelessly ugly and inferior to the pigeon." He paused. We leaned into his story. He smiled and continued, "In fact, they made him feel so insecure about himself that he would now do anything just to become a pigeon."

He paused again to give our imaginations the time to visualize the characters; and, since he had not described the peacock or the pigeon, Sunny had succeeded at reaching into our imaginations and pulling out our personal images of the characters, images each of us could understand and relate to, succeeding at telling everyone a slightly different story at the same time. "So the pigeons," he continued, "convinced the peacock to pluck all his feathers and hand them over to them, which he did in earnest. The pigeons laughed and sold his treasure at the bazaar for, needless to say, a handsome sum. Still not finished with the peacock, they forced him to replace his graceful walk with the jerky pigeon gait." He stopped his story to act out the different walks.

As he jerked about, countless thoughts flooded our minds. I don't know about the others, but my first thought was of a farmer who gives up his land to work in a factory. I thought about the man who gives up the world for a few miserly possessions that some "pigeon" told him was how civilized people lived. Then, I thought about the doctor and shook my head. Sunny ceased his walk, fell into a squat, and continued, "The peacock then turned his beak up on all his kind, cut and stole all their feathers while they were asleep, and returned to live with the pigeons who greedily took the treasures he had stolen, and, having no more real use for him, paid him the two pigeon feathers and had him attend to all the dirty and humiliating tasks of the village. Now, the peacock did all this work because the pigeons had convinced him he was one of them. But when he was banned from entering all the fun and beautiful huts in the village, he quickly realized he would never be one of them, and that they would continue to humiliate and abuse him so long as tried to be like them. So he threw his pigeon feathers to the ground and returned to his village. But when he returned, the peacocks, remembering his crime, refused to take him back." Sunny finished as he always did, gazing into our eyes, searching, one by one, to see if his story had taken root in our minds. This time he wasn't disappointed. A deathly silence fell over us as we all knew someone who had served a "pigeon" and who had, regrettably, spilled "peacock" blood.

May 10

Under a dark and threatening sky, and over a calm and peaceful ocean, we glided smoothly, making steady progress toward what many are now calling the "Golden Mountains". Dreams, golden dreams are all I hear people discussing day in and out as I walk by clusters of friends fiercely animated in discussions about the families they left behind, and of the prosperous days to come. At night, when everyone was asleep and Amar struggled with his dreams, Sunny turned to me and said, "You awake?" "No," was my answer. I turned to him with a smile and we shared a silent laugh. He said, "I can't wait to smell Canada." "Me too," I said, and then repeated in a whisper, "Me too." He continued with emotion, "To smell the grass and trees, the mountains and rivers, the people and places; to see a new sky and touch new land…" I nodded and added, "Me too." He continued, "Giving and generous land; land so generous that our stomachs will never be empty and…and when the King comes to rob our plates, we won't even feel it." I nodded slightly. "We won't," I said. There was a short silence. Then he broke the silence. "I miss my family," he said, with his eyes turned inward. I closed my eyes slowly. "Me too," I said softly, and we fell silent.

May 11

The weather plays games with us. The day began warm and hopeful; but as evening descended, the sky turned grey and clouded over, and the sea held its breath, turning into a motionless black sheet. We found security below deck and waited for the storm to come, but no storm came. And now, to add to our anxieties, someone has started a terrible rumour that we may not be able to land in Canada. It is a foolish thought that I try not to pay attention to. How can British authorities stop British subjects from setting foot on British soil?

May 12

Apparently the doctor started the rumour. I saw him arguing with Gurdit near the engine room. For a short while they forgot their lofty learned language and yelled in their native Punjabi. Gurdit accused the doctor of trying to destroy the morale of Nanak Jahaz, and told him to stop putting negative thoughts into his passengers. In the evening, Gurdit herded us on deck and told us what we all already knew: that to keep British subjects out of Canada would be a crime against the King; an act of anarchy in an Empire where all British subjects are allowed free movement. Everyone soon realized the absurdity of the doctor's words and quickly went back to their joviality.

At night I was awakened by Amar who shook and shouted in his sleep. Sweat slipped down his face and then tears streamed down his cheeks and disappeared into his thick black beard. He shifted and mumbled desperate apologies to someone or something only he could see in the chaos of his mind. Sunny nudged me, and we both observed him with concern. All of a sudden Amar woke with a cry. We instantly shut our eyes, feigning a deep and undisturbed sleep. Then, he rose slowly and quietly snuck on deck. He spent the entire night there.

May 13

Today a funny thing happened. In the morning, after filling ourselves with Waheguru's name, we took our morning meal on deck and were subsequently interrupted by a shy yet courageous crewman, who approached us with a plate bearing slivers of raw fish. He stood before us for a moment and we ceased our chewing and looked up at him with questioning looks. Unbothered by our gazes, he sat beside Sanjay, crossed his legs, and smiled with the biggest smile I have ever seen in my life. And his smile was the key into our circle. He proceeded to show us his plate, offering each of us a sliver of fish. Sadly, none of us had the courage to try it, and the two brothers began to argue over who would dare to try the Japanese delicacy. Ali refused and swore he would wash Sanjay's clothes for five days if he'd eat the fish. And so, much to the crewman's pleasure, Sanjay took a piece and, after a long meditation, thrust the pinkish-orange sliver into his mouth. I must say, that was the longest I have ever seen Sanjay chew anything. He made horrible, inappropriate, and, in my opinion, highly offensive faces until he realized the crewman was watching gravely. Then, he put on an act and rubbed his stomach, moaning with intense pleasure as if it were the best thing he had ever eaten in his life.

The crewman smiled and gestured for him to exchange meals with him. Sanjay shook his head vigorously and tried to explain in Punjabi how he needed his daal-rotis for a healthy and productive day. The crewman refused to take no for an answer. Eventually, Sanjay surrendered to the man's persistence and cheer and reluctantly handed over his plate. We, as you can imagine, laughed like bells! He gave us a dirty look and then proceeded to show the crewman how to eat with rotis, tearing off a triangle, scooping some daal, then dipping it in yoghurt. The crewman took a bite and paused, his eyes watered and widened, his lips began to tremble, and his nostrils flared; then, faster than a rabbit with its tail on fire, he reached for our cups and drank all of our water and tea. It

27

must have been too spicy for his palate. But the man was braver than Sanjay and finished his food despite the beads of sweat pouring down his face. We spent the rest of the morning watching Sanjay with great amusement as he attempted to empty his plate. When he finally finished, the crewman smiled his fantastic smile, wiped the sweat off his glistening face, gave Sanjay a hearty and congratulatory pat on the back, and went back to his station with quick, cheery steps. I think Sanjay is the first Punjabi to have ever eaten raw fish!

May 14

Dawn broke, warm and pleasant, and, as we ate our morning meal, the crewman came to exchange meals with Sanjay again. And again his persistence paid off. I think he enjoys Indian food. This time he came prepared with some rice and water, which he undoubtedly used to put out the fire in his mouth. He introduced himself as Naki and earnestly tried to communicate with us. We only understood what he was trying to say when Gurdit happened to pass by and translated; apparently he's been taking Japanese lessons from the captain. I much admire Gurdit's passion for other cultures.

Gurdit told us that Naki was trying to communicate we were lucky to be British subjects and that he wished he too could live in Canada. Then I thought I'd try to explain that the only reason we had to leave our homes was because of what the British had done to our country: how they had raped our land; how they robbed us of all our natural resources to build and strengthen their own country while they weakened ours; and how they gave us the status of British subject solely to appease our anger while they continue their abuse without fear of revolt or rebellion. If they are destroying our country, at least it is for an Empire to which we all belong, or at least, this is the attitude that keeps us quiet. Though, really, I'd trade places with this young Japanese man any time just to have my own country; to have my father and brother here with me even for but a second. But instead they are dead; they died defending a faceless King who keeps us silent with the promise of belonging. So I feel no guilt for Naki. He has not earned the right in blood and hunger to the opportunities we are entitled to in Canada.

In the afternoon Ali washed Sanjay's clothes and swore it was all worth it because, when he saw his wife and children again, he would tell them Sanjay had eaten raw fish. But as soon as the thought of home entered his mind, his smile faded and his head sank and silence stole over him. He left a wife and two little girls behind, and Sanjay, like me, left a wife and a boy. At night Amar struggled in his sleep and sought refuge from his nightmares in the sea. This time I threaded my way around the sleeping passengers and climbed on deck to watch him. He leaned over the rail and stared at the dark abyss below without noticing me. I don't know what he saw there, but I'm certain I heard him cry. I stood beside him and asked if he was okay, or if he needed to talk, but he just stuck out his hand, and, without turning to face me, motioned for me to go away. I understood his need to be alone and left him, though I know that, at times, it is damaging to be alone, to be always alone.

May 15

The sun rose and embraced Nanak Jahaz with warm arms. The passengers were on deck gazing at the horizon, or the sky, or the sea, or else they were playing games: some raced from bow to stern, others played kabadi, and one passenger, tall and thick, demonstrated the immense strength of his mouth by tying one end of a rope to a lifeboat and placing the other end in his mouth and then dragging the vessel with the sheer strength of his jaw and neck. His face was so red I thought he was going to explode! But he succeeded at moving it about five feet and everyone, including the Japanese crewmen, marvelled at and cheered his strength. Naki came down from the housing above to excitedly shake the man's hand while he praised him in a language no one could understand. Then he jumped into the lifeboat and signalled for the passenger to pull him. The passenger shook his head, smiled a hearty smile, and took the rope in his mouth. And, sure enough, he pulled the lifeboat with Naki inside it. Unexpectedly, two other passengers jumped in and, seemingly undaunted, he pulled them, too. Soon the lifeboat was filled with excited passengers, laughing and hollering for him to pull them. I have never seen such strength.

In the evening I was entertained by Ali and Sanjay who competed over who could eat the most peppers without drinking a single drop of water. Ali has a gigantic leather purse filled with red and green peppers which his wife prepared for him because she believed they didn't have peppers in Canada. Ali went on to explain that these were the hottest peppers ever grown in the Punjab, and, of course, Sanjay scoffed at his words. Ali swore Sanjay couldn't bear even one, and Sanjay retorted he could bear a lot more than Ali could. One challenge led to another, and soon enough, they were each swallowing one pepper after another, stubbornly waiting to see who would give in first. They must have finished half the bag before Sanjay, looking as if he were on fire, gave up. Ali ate about five more after Sanjay quit, just to prove some unknown point. Now they are even and Ali doesn't have to wash his clothes anymore. At least, for the time being.

May 18

I am weak and have little energy. Something terrible happened to me and you nearly lost your father. Sunny watches over me and so do the others; but Sanjay and Ali leave me every now and then to go watch the horizon. They have another game going: whoever sees land first gets his house built by the other in Canada. When Sunny told me, weak as I was, I laughed and wasn't in the least surprised. I will write more when I am stronger.

May 19

A few days ago, a storm unlike any I have ever experienced pounded us like a furious fist. It beat and shook and shocked us straight out of our dreams. It played a cruel game with our ship, throwing and tossing it around like a toy boat as everyone held fast to anything secure or bolted. The wind howled and cut the water like a tree. Tree after tree crashed mercilessly over the upper deck as men below were thrown into walls, latrines, bunks, each other. I held onto my bunk as tightly as I could and watched the moon-lit water pour down the companionway. Scanning around, I saw Ali and Sunny and Sanjay, each holding their respective benches, eyes wide with terror and faces white with fear. That's when I noticed Amar's empty bunk. I gasped and quickly sensed the danger and heard within my heart a soft cry for help. For a brief moment I felt the coward within me emerge seeking any excuse to ignore the peril of the man above, and that coward found every reason to stay safe and secure below. That coward even used you as an excuse. He tried to convince me that I couldn't risk my life for another because I was a family man; a father; a responsible father with a son to raise and a wife to take care of; and that it would be selfish of me to go above and risk my life for some man I hardly knew.

Shame on me for such cowardly thoughts! Shame on me for using my family as an excuse for inaction. Shame on me for fearing death. Inaction when action is required is never justified, no matter how hard the coward within attempts to rationalize it. Son, be wary of that coward, for he is clever and can rationalize anything. And so, without another thought, I summoned my courage, and with Waheguru strong in my heart and the strength of my ancestors running through my veins, I lunged toward the companionway.

With cries and pleas from my beloved friends echoing behind me, I battled my way up the ladder. The silver seawater proved a worthy adversary, throwing me down several times and twice almost rendering me unconscious. But I kept on going and eventually I succeeded; though I had no time to rejoice, for as soon as I took my fist step on deck the wind blasted me and threw me to the ground, ripping my turban off my head. My hair flew wildly in all directions. I crawled toward the rail where, through the moonlit spray, I caught a glimpse of Amar flattened over the deck--either unconscious or dead--with his arms hanging over the side. I pushed my way toward him with the wind screaming in my ears. I had nearly reached him when, out of nowhere, a mountain of water crashed over me and threw me ten feet back. My lungs filled with its salty water. I spat and coughed until my lungs were empty, and then I searched for Amar to no avail. I prayed he hadn't been swept overboard and, contrary to my better judgement, I rose with difficulty so that I could

31

better search the ship. Waves crashed over me and swept the deck from bow to stern. The ship trembled to its very core, but I maintained my balance and resolve. Eventually I spotted him. Through the silver spray and madness I saw him sprawled across the deck just a few feet from where I had first seen him. I chanced a step forward, but no sooner did I place my foot down than a wave, immeasurable and pitiless, crashed down over me, slammed me into the hard deck, and in an instant lifted me straight back up and thrust me overboard!

But Waheguru was watching over me; as I somersaulted overboard, my hair tangled in the rail and kept me from falling into the raging sea. I could feel my hair ripping at the scalp under my weight. When I realized I had been saved, I took the few seconds Waheguru had blessed me with to grab the rail and hold on for dear life. I tried my best, with the water and wind against me, to lift myself over the rail, but it was no use, there wasn't a drop of strength left in me. Nevertheless, refusing to give up, I calmed my breathing and closed my eyes and meditated on Waheguru's name; then, opening my eyes with renewed determination, I pulled my torso half way over the rail. Struggling against the unrelenting wind, I had almost pulled myself over when some strange metal object came flying at me, struck me in the head, and knocked me unconscious.

When I gained consciousness and opened my heavy eyes, I was surrounded by my friends and Amar was lying safe and unconscious beside me. They laughed and called me crazy and told me that they had made an unbreakable chain and had caught me right before the dark and unforgiving sea could devour me. I smiled as best as I could, murmured my gratitude, and drifted into a beautiful dream that carried me back home.

May 20

The sun shone over the ocean as Nanak Jahaz cut though the glassy blue Pacific and brought us closer and closer to land. When you've been out at sea for as long as we have, the slightest change in air causes strange and inexpressible feelings inside, and makes you constantly search the horizon for land. Now many of us miss meals just to be the first one to see a mountain, a tree, or a bird.

I am stronger now and walking around the ship with a whole new sensibility. Everything seems different in ways I can hardly explain. My eyes seem more open than they've ever been, and I'm seeing things I've never noticed before. It's almost like I've been blessed with a new set of eyes--a new set of senses! I smell things I've never smelled before but knew were always there: the odour of condensed humanity all around me; the scent of onion and garlic and ginger infused in our clothes and blankets; the fresh sea air that drifts down the companionway and spreads over our bunks to freshen our spirits.

Then there are the sounds. There are many. Sounds I've never noticed before. Now I hear everything, and not just as a jumble of sounds, but as sounds in concert, sounds in distinct layers that work together to produce the symphony of the ship: the soft and subtle but ever-present breathing sea; the monotonous, bass drone of the steam engine; the pitter-patter of men moving around the deck; the stories and whispers of homesick men all around me; Sunny and Ali and Sanjay breathing beside me.

And then there are my observations and thoughts. There are things I've never before observed, considered, or even thought of going through my mind. Today, for instance, I watched the passengers, I examined their faces, and it suddenly occurred to me that some men seemed more alive than others. And then I wondered if, indeed, some men were more alive than others and what it was that made one man more alive than another. I wondered if it was something as simple as an attitude, or a state of mind; a way of looking at one's life and situation. And then I thought about Sunny and the doctor and I thought that it quite possibly had everything to do with attitude: that some men want so much and yet enjoy so little, while others have so little and yet enjoy so much. This can only be a matter of mind.

Sanjay enjoys Japanese food now and, without a fuss, exchanges plates as soon as he sees Naki. Ali absolutely refuses to budge from the rail where he spends all his time searching the horizon, determined to see land before Sanjay. Sanjay isn't worried, not in the least; he's got a strong and reliable team searching for him; he's promised a piggyback ride around the ship to the first boy who sees land and tells him about it without alarming Ali.

In the evening, as the sun slipped behind the horizon and illuminated each and every cloud with a thousand and one shades of yellow, orange, and pink, Gurdit herded the passengers on deck and thanked everyone for being so pleasant and cooperative during the voyage. He told us that we'd be reaching Canada any time now and that he expected us to look our best when we walked off the ship. At his wonderful words, great emotions stirred within all of us and soon we were all hollering and cheering our irrepressible joy. The only one who wasn't celebrating was Amar, which wasn't much of a surprise; he still hasn't thanked me for trying to save his life. Maybe he doesn't know. In any case, the journey is almost over and I will leave Nanak Jahaz with three wonderful friends to whom I owe my life. Only Waheguru knows how much they mean to me.

May 21

Land! Land! Land! At last, land! In the pearly and mystic time between night and dawn, Gurdit's boy spotted the first glimpse of land and rushed down the companionway, zigzagged and leapt over snoring men, and shook Sanjay wide awake. Sanjay woke to the boy's excited face, and he whispered, "Land?" The boy nodded breathlessly and smiled, and his smile spread to Sanjay's face. The boy, in his excitement, had woken up a few other passengers, and soon a small procession followed Sanjay to the upper deck. Though we still couldn't see anything yet, the sweet smell of land greeted us with open arms. We knew we had arrived. Some even took exaggerated breaths and savoured each and every new sensation dancing through their sleepy bodies.

Unfortunately, Ali had fallen asleep by the rail, so we made a small crescent around him as we squinted with difficulty through the misty air, searching desperately for the place from where all those wonderful new smells came. Sunny was the first to see the great black shadows. His big chubby cheeks rose in a smile, and he began to shout and scream his happiness, regardless of those who were still sleeping. Uncontrollable happiness jumped into all of our faces, joy welled in our

34

hearts, and our eyes and brows danced together as one. My skin prickled from the excitement. Sunny's jaw dropped, his eyes squinted, and he released a full-throated laugh. The next thing I knew, he was twirling me and screaming to the world that his family would be so proud of him and that they would never again know the meaning of hunger. And would you believe Ali slept through the entire racket, only awaking when he heard the unfamiliar voice of some strange bird singing in the distance! He must have exhausted himself searching for land, straining his eyes to the point of hypnosis, so that even if he had been awake and looking directly at land he would have probably still missed it. There's something hypnotic about the sea so that if you gaze at its silvery surface for too long, you no longer see water, but life, your life, and the events of forgotten days unfold before you like a dream and, before you know it, you've spent the entire day gazing inward and you wonder where all the time went.

Ali woke and stood without a word; not a single measure of disappointment could be read in his face. I looked at him waiting for a sigh or a grunt or a disappointed moan, but his face betrayed not a single frustration for having lost the game; there was only happiness for a dream half realized. Sanjay put his hand on his friend's shoulder and said, "I hope you build better than you clean!" After a short silence, the two exploded into gales of laughter and from Ali's eye slipped a tear of joy.

The only one who didn't come up to see the land was Amar. He remained below, hiding from the warmth and merriment above, staring solemnly at his certificate. I descended, approached him, sat cross-legged beside him, and subsequently shared my excitement with him. He regarded me a moment, then his gaze dropped back to his certificate, and he said, "We haven't landed yet." I shook my head at him, stood, and left him in his misery, returning to where the air was fresh and clean and filled with the smell of land and the heart-soothing laughter of men.

The sun rose and poured its golden waters over us. I stood beside Sanjay and we watched the land with the others. Then Gurdit's boy came with his two followers by his side and tugged on Sanjay's jacket. Sanjay turned and, remembering his promise, threw the boy to his shoulders and headed toward the stern. Then another boy went to Ali and tugged on his jacket. Without hesitation, Ali followed suit. I was about to put the doctor's boy on my shoulders when the doctor yelled at him from his cabin and admonished him for being in the sun, demanding that he return to the cabin before he turned a degree darker.

The boy's chin dropped to his chest and he plodded to his father's cabin muttering something foul under an angry breath. Sunny looked at me and shook his head at the doctor's inferiority complex; then he approached me and said, "Maybe if he keeps him under the bed he'll eventually turn into a paleface." We laughed at the doctor's fears and promised one another that we'd never be ashamed of our skin colour, and that, no matter how hard the British tried to contaminate us with their books and newspapers and conventions, trying their best to inspire inse-curities and inadequacies in our thoughts, we'd always remain large-hearted, sun-loving Punjabi farmers. Sunny and I watched Ali and Sanjay race each other with screaming and laughing boys straddled on their shoulders. Wanting to join the fun, Sunny jumped on my back and demanded we race toward them. And race toward them we did!

At sunset, a Canadian pilot boarded the ship and guided him to a place where, the next morning, he said he would examine him. Now no one can sleep for eagerness and excitement, and Sunny is frantically searching the ship for someone to help him tie his bright yellow necktie, which his elder brother gave him so that he would look his best when he reached Canada. But none of us know how to tie a necktie and he may have to settle with an improvisation. Neckties are ridiculous things any-way; they're just another way the British have managed to complicate our lives. If we hadn't been so trained to see it as a symbol of prestige and success, one might actually consider a piece of cloth dangling from one's jugular to be quite absurd, as absurd as eating daal-roti with a fork and knife.

Now I'm shivering with excitement to disembark. I have heard from others who have been out to sea before that, when you disembark after several weeks at sea it is hard to keep your balance on land. They said the ground feels as though it is breathing, rolling, rising, and falling just like the sea. Apparently, it will take several days to readjust to a sta-ble life and I may even find myself sick and disorientated. I find it remarkable how a man can get used to any situation so that, in the end, the one he knew from birth suddenly becomes foreign and strange to all his senses. I actually look forward to stumbling over my feet. I miss you, my son.

May 22

This morning, Sanjay, much to his surprise and approval, received the extra rotis, daal, and yoghurt he's been asking for the whole way here. The cooks just smiled at him and gave him double the portion. They said that it wasn't a problem as there were two or three days worth of provisions left and we'd be disembarking tomorrow. We were all allowed seconds but most of us were content with what was put on our plate. Sanjay searched for Naki, but to no avail. Either Sanjay is fond of fish or he is fond of Naki, and I'm inclined to believe he is fond of both.

As we finished our food, a medical officer boarded and gave Nanak Jahaz a thorough inspection. It took all day, and when the quarantine medical officer completed his inspection, Gurdit herded the passengers on deck to tell us that there would be one more quick medical examination and that we'd soon be on our way. He went on to explain how we didn't have to worry about the examination, as it was fairly routine and that, for British subjects, the immigration medical officer usually went through three hundred passengers in about an hour, and that the officer merely touched your forehead to check for fever and then asked you a fairly simple question to make sure you were neither deaf nor dumb; then, if your temperature was normal and you answered the question properly, you were on your way. Besides, Gurdit explained, the quarantine officer had told him that he was impressed with the general cleanliness of the ship and the excellent health of the passengers. He had expected much worse conditions after such a long and turbulent voyage, and that, more often than not, he had to keep ships like ours in quarantine for weeks. I thank Waheguru that we weren't quarantined. I don't think I can bear ship life much longer, and I can't wait to set foot on solid land; to sleep on solid ground; and, more than ever, to sink my hands in the ground and let the earth run down my arms. I also need another blanket. It's so cold here that I probably couldn't bear another night without a good blanket.

37

After congratulating Gurdit on a job well done, the Canadian pilot took control of the ship and guided it to Vancouver. As the ship slipped gently across the sea, we waited in line for our vaccination shots. That's when I discovered how afraid Sunny was of needles. Every time we got closer and closer to the ship's doctor, he dragged me back to the end of the line! And he kept doing this until I refused to go back. As the doctor sank the needle into his arm, I had to hold his other hand, look him straight in the eye, and assure him that nothing catastrophic was going to happen to him. The doctor then smiled at us. I think that was the first time I had ever seen him smile. Either he likes to administer pain or he's in high spirits like everyone else. I want to believe he's in high spirits as, right now, everyone is practically exploding with excitement, except for maybe one man, and he's not even worth mentioning. Now I have to go prepare my stuff and probably won't be in a position to write for a few days, as there will be much to do as I settle into my new life. Most of the passengers are already on board with their bags by their sides, holding the rail and staring at the coastline like children discovering the world for the very first time. I love and miss you with all my heart.

May 23

No one can sleep for cold, confusion, and despair. We need food and more blankets! They won't let us disembark and no one understands why; though we all suspect that it might have something to do with the colour of our skin. There is nothing more to write except words of anger and hate, foul and despicable words, words unworthy of your time. And so, I will refrain from putting these dark thoughts to paper until my mind is clear and my heart is free. Waheguru stay with me.

May 24

The shores are shadowy. Fringed with tall and stately trees that spread their green over waters shrouded in mist, the true face of this place is well camouflaged under natural masks of deceptive beauty. Sunny won't budge from the rail. He's been there for two days, staring at the shore like a man who has lost everything and has nothing left to live for. His eyes lack life; they have abandoned hope and embraced defeat. I can see a hard shell drawing over him. I can see a hard shell drawing over all of us.

We're floating at anchor about two hundred yards away from the pier, but no one would dare jump overboard as none of us know how to swim, and, even if we did, the water is as cold as ice. Nevertheless, an immigration patrol boat circles us just in case one of us tries to escape. The patrol boat has already stopped a boat filled with local Indians, friends of Gurdit, from approaching our ship. They have also placed an official on Nanak Jahaz, and he doesn't want to be here any more than we want him here.

This place is cold, but not nearly as cold as the immigration officials who boarded our ship yesterday and those angry men who sing some strange song on shore. I wonder what they're singing. They're using the power of poetry and song to rouse their anger and hate. They seem so angry and fearful you can almost see the anger and fear rising from them like a gigantic thunderhead ready to release its torrent on us. I tried to pull Sunny away from the rail today, but he wouldn't budge. Holding his tie in his hand, he just stares at the shore in silence, gazing at the angry mob hollering dark words at us, gazing at them with wet, confused eyes, trying hard to understand the past few days and why those men seem to hate us so much.

They say we cannot land, yet they give no reason. It all happened so fast. We rounded the inlet and before we knew it, we were anchored far away from the pier. Immigration officers, clad in perfectly pressed uniforms, came aboard and stared at us with cold eyes. A passenger came up beside me and pointed to one of the officers. He said his name was Hopkinson; he had heard many stories about him. Hopkinson was tall and clean-shaven, and he wore the malicious grin of a man who thought himself better than everyone else. The passenger continued to tell me that there were rumours that Hopkinson's mother was Indian, that he despised her, and that because he despised his mother he despised all Indians, and because he despised all Indians he would do anything to keep the race out of his part of the Empire. When you look at him it's hard to see even the slightest degree of Indian in him. He's as pale as his sense of truth and justice. And when he attempts to speak our language you almost want to laugh. And some of us did laugh, which humiliated him and caused him to turn red with rage and gaze at us as if he were ready to slaughter us all right then and there. We must be careful because I think he's convinced his superiors that he can speak our language. Maybe that's the only reason he has a job. In any case, there was another officer who tried to speak Punjabi, but he might as well have been a duck for we couldn't understand him any better than Hopkinson. It's almost insulting to hear them butcher our language. If their faces weren't so serious you would think they were trying to insult us. Luckily, Gurdit speaks English; but who knows, maybe he doesn't speak English any better than these men speak Punjabi. I wouldn't know. It seems to me that when Gurdit speaks, the officers understand because they answer and acknowledge him. Whereas, when Hopkinson or the other man speaks, we all look at one another wondering if anyone had deciphered any meaning from the mutilated words.

The passenger then pointed to another immigration officer, who was stoic and unsmiling, and who seemed to be the man in charge. He told me that he didn't know who he was, but that his moustache was the funniest thing he had ever seen in his life. It was thick and waxed and curled, and so we decided to call him "Moustache." He spoke with Gurdit and, the whole time, he stared at him with a calm smile. Then, suddenly, amidst a peaceful talk, they broke into an argument, and no sooner did they begin raising their voices than Gurdit exploded into a terrible rage. I have never seen Gurdit so upset. Knowing him, you wouldn't think it possible. His words are gentle and well-considered, and he usually lets you do all the talking. But he was, for the first time since I met him, out of control. The two leaders yelled at each other and only stopped when Moustache turned his back on Gurdit and returned to his launch, leaving us stranded in the sea.

Gurdit went to his room with his son and only came back when he was of a calmer and more secure face. When he returned, he faced men filled to their eyes with despair and confusion; he told us that we may encounter some difficulties entering this dominion, as the gatekeepers of this part of the Empire were uncaring anarchists who refuse to obey the laws of their King. He said that he had not foreseen these unfortunate events and that he would hire a lawyer to help us.

May 25

Gurdit and the doctor had an argument today in front of everyone. No
one really knows what it was about as they were yelling in English, but
many think the doctor blames Gurdit for the mess we're in. Though,
much to his disappointment, he would be the only one. No one else
blames Gurdit for anything. He's just trying to do the best he can for us,
and is, after all, following British law, while the officers we saw yesterday still haven't told us why they've decided to detain us. We are prisoners of this cold sea, but have committed no crime: unless it is a crime to
want to do the best for our families. If that is a crime, I am guilty. We are
all guilty. If the doctor is upset, he should be arguing with the real criminals.

 A strange thing is that the crewmen are allowed to go ashore, and
they aren't even subjects of the Empire. But Gurdit says this is because
they are trying to convince the captain to take the ship back. He then
assured us that we had nothing to worry about, that he and the captain
had become close friends, and that he would always swear by the captain
as a man of character and integrity. He went on to say that if the immigration officials were more like the captain, and less like gangsters, we
would already be in Canada.

 In the evening, as the sun sank behind the mountains, and filled
the world with a glorious beauty none of us could perceive, I managed to
pull Sunny from the rail. He was too weak to put up a struggle. He merely dropped his necktie in the water and followed me to the lower deck. I
gave him the small piece of roti I had saved from this morning as I knew
he would need the nourishment more than me. He hadn't eaten for days
and had missed the only piece of rotis we were allowed. I wish he would
talk. I wish more people would talk. The silence on the ship is deafening.
Waheguru, stay with us. Keep us strong and together.

May 26

Today I discovered something terrible about the mob that sings and hollers and cheers against us on the pier. They are awful words; it is an awful song; a song I'd rather not put to paper; but, so that you may know the minds of these men, I will.

I was watching the pier, observing the angry mob with Sunny when Gurdit approached us from behind, startling us. "If you knew what they were singing," he said sadly, placing his hand on the rail, "your heart would break." His eyes set on the mob and his body went rigid. As we continued to watch the men, he sighed and continued, "They are singing a song called 'White Canada Forever.' I know this because the captain brought a newspaper aboard." He sighed again and we just stared at the men screaming and spitting their venom at us. "If you had read the articles about us, your blood would boil and your anger would rise to the heavens that they would say such things." I turned to him and asked what they were singing. He shook his head slowly and began to sing the dark words in our tongue, "Oh brave men, let us stand together; and show our father's might; that won the home we call our own; for white man's land we fight! To Oriental grasp and greed we'll never surrender; Our watchword be God Save The King; White Canada forever."

I listened to those words and wondered if we were Orientals. I wondered if they were referring to the same King my father and brother died for; and then I wondered if they were referring to the same King whose laws they were breaking. There was a long moment of silence, then Gurdit, breaking the silence, said, "That is not how everyone thinks. It's what the officials want them to think. It is a form of opinion control. They pay actors to line the shore and attract a crowd so that they can spread their fear and hatred and get the whole country against us." He paused for a moment, shook his head, and sighed. Then he whispered, "If you knew what they wrote about us, your blood would boil." Sunny turned to Gurdit and spoke for the first time since we became prisoners of the sea. He said in a voice full of anguish, "What will happened to my family?" Gurdit put his hand on his shoulder and said, "I don't know…but, by the grace of Waheguru, I will do my best to right this wrong." When I looked into his eyes I saw steel, and as I searched deeper, I saw determination, the determination of a leader who would give his head to the tyrant before he surrendered. Gurdit returned to his cabin to meet with the passengers committee and we spent the day watching the spectacle on the pier.

I stared at them, profoundly saddened and sickened by the sight. I was shocked, and as the day progressed, my heart filled with a deep sorrow and my mind assailed me with a thousand and one different questions: questions on men, on character, on integrity. How could men sing such things? How could they sing such things and not even mean them! They are cheap men. They are cheap men who sell their emotions, their thoughts, their characters for a miserly pittance. They are soulless. These are the men we are dealing with. And even though I knew this spectacle before me was nothing more than cheap theatre, nothing more than carefully rehearsed speeches, tried and memorized hate rhetoric, it struck my soul down to think that these so-called civilised men were capable of such barbarity; that these men, whose fathers were once like us, traveling to a new world with dreams and hopes for the betterment of their families, would willingly spread a plague of fear and hate to help the officials pound the humanity out of us. What theatre! What horrible and most cruel theatre! Cruel actors! Cruel actors playing to a cruel audience who transform this country into a cruel place, all in a horrible and most effective attempt to deprive us of our humanity. We are dealing with well-put-together barbarians, necktie-wearing barbarians clad in finely made suits who use convention and complicated phrases to camouflage their true savage faces. I am upset. I should stop writing. I love you. Waheguru, stay with us; save our minds from the plague.

Most of the actors vanished last night. Either the officials could no longer afford them, or they've done their job and Vancouver is irreversibly infected. Hate and fear will open the floodgates of hell, and we should expect the worst. Gurdit translated an article for us and it seems as though Vancouver is in a state of panic as they prepare for a Hindu invasion. Imagine that! A Hindu invasion! As a joke, some of us pretended to search the sea for the Hindu Armada, but no such armada came. There are only ten or fifteen men of the Hindu faith on Nanak Jahaz, and so they must be referring to another ship. But, in truth, we know that Hindus, Muslims, and Sikhs are all Hindus to them.

To them a Hindu is not a man who practices a particular faith, but a man who hasn't a drop of humanity within him. It's an easy word to remember for the plague-stricken men and women of Vancouver, who believe everything they read in the newspapers and who question little, as they, busy with their lives, care little for particulars but much for fabricated generalities. At least we've kept or, rather, refused to part with our sense of humour, for humour is most empowering, and humour is and always will be the greatest weapon against despair: it helps us maintain our dignity and self-respect; it aids us in our struggle for self-preservation; it helps us forget the cold and hunger that weakens us day by day; and, most importantly, it reminds us that we are not animals, as the newspapers would like everyone to believe, but that we are, in fact, thinking beings with free and clever minds capable of brilliant tricks to help us escape our worries--even if that escape is only for a brief moment. So long as we can still laugh, we have not been defeated. So long as we can still laugh, we have maintained our integrity, our dignity, our self-respect, our humanity.

But there is something no passenger here dares to joke about. The officials won't let Gurdit speak to a lawyer, which is a terrible violation of his rights--our rights! But then again, do monsters have rights? I suppose they don't. Do the men and women of Vancouver care about the Hindu? Probably not. They've been infected by the words they've allowed into their minds and now they hide in the comfort of their homes, praying that the heroic immigration officers will continue to keep the Hindus at bay.

How can they do this? What kind of officers are they? They are not gangsters: they are communists! Only a communist official would break the very laws he was elected to maintain. Only a communist would hire actors to sing with acid tongues. Only communists would turn Sikhs and Muslims and Hindus into gun-waving, fire-breathing invaders. But, then again, when I think about it, all I've ever heard about communists I've learned through the newspapers; and now that I see the evil of these papers, I wonder if what I read about them was true.

Maybe the communists were our monster: the monster the British needed to keep us fearful and to justify spending all of our taxes on an already great and undefeated military, while we watched our children starve. Maybe the British were trying to shape our opinions about the communist as they are trying to mould the minds of the good citizens of this colony. For if the people of Vancouver saw us as human, they would never stand for the way immigration is treating us.

If there is such a thing as evil, the newspapers are nothing short. Is there anything more evil than fiction parading itself as non-fiction? It is through this evil device that the tyrant may cleverly control his subjects. I say to you now, my son, never believe anything they write about us in the papers. It is either flat-out false, or selectively chosen to destroy the credibility and integrity of the men aboard this ship. Our cause is noble, our cause is just, and our cause is legal. But, most important, we are not invaders. Your father, no matter what you read, is not an invader, for to be an invader you would first have to be an alien. I will put the journal down as I feel the anger within me rising. I will not write for a day or so as I will be praying; I seek Waheguru's warmth, guidance, and wisdom. There is a reason this is happening to us. There is always a reason. I wish I knew what that reason was.

May 31

The captain snuck some blankets on board; he has a good heart. The children are amusing themselves at the expense of the guard placed on board to watch us. They make faces at him, tap him, and throw things at him, trying to get some kind of reaction out of him, but he's like a sentinel, and they might as well be teasing a statue. He is too scared to move, though you see times when he clearly wished he were alone with his young bullies. Gurdit calls the boys away every now and then and admonishes them for bothering the officer; but as soon as he returns to his room to meet with the passengers committee, the boys go straight back to their victim, amusing themselves immensely.

I have also recently learned some terrible news. A week ago, as we approached Vancouver, Naki jumped ship and made a desperate swim for the "Golden Mountains." Many think he drowned. Waheguru be with him. He was a good man with a kind and adventurous soul. I don't know how to tell Sanjay who, in the last few days, has more than once searched for his Japanese friend.

June 1

No more food. Only water. Many of us are sick and weak. No one, save the children, do anything but lie around Nanak Jahaz, hiding in the shade, conserving vital energy. The captain and the crewmen try to help us as best as they can, but we are over three hundred passengers and there is only so much they can sneak aboard. As long as they keep the passengers committee healthy and strong we will be all right.

Now Ali and Sanjay spend all their time standing by the rail, staring at a patrol boat where two immigration officers stand on deck, supervising us as if we were caged beasts plotting an escape. Sometimes they point at us and laugh, and their despicable laughter floats up to our ship and sinks into our hearts, adding to our despair. As defence, as a way to combat their subtle attacks, Ali and Sanjay have devised a game that keeps their minds off of their hunger and humiliation. They lean over the rail and stare at the patrol boat, assign themselves an officer to mimic, and then observe their lips waiting for movement. When their assigned officer speaks, they make up their own dialogue, and the winner of the game is the one who maintains the continuity of the conversation, the one who can continue the dialogue without stumbling or hesitating over his words. By the end of the day, three or four other men, tired of their

46

despair, joined the game, and, even in their weakened condition, found something to laugh at. The officers watched us return their laughter and were silenced.

June 2

There is no longer a guard on this ship. Gurdit, furious that one had attacked his boy last night, swore to the immigration officers that they had better start treating us like human beings and that, until they did, they would not be allowed to come aboard. Moustache laughed at Gurdit's threat, but Gurdit assured him that any immigration officer placed on board overnight would, without apology, be thrown overboard! Gurdit then attempted to explain what had taken place the night before, but Moustache refused to listen and said he would only listen to his man's version of the story since he had little or no trust for the Hindu, which is not surprising.

I didn't see what happened, but Ali did, and, as we all watched Gurdit argue with Moustache, he explained, "Last night the boy was fooling around, making strange faces at the paleface, and you could see that the paleface was becoming more and more agitated by the boy's folly. The boy was slowly getting under his skin and I think he wanted to do something to stop the boy from bothering him, but there was always someone lingering about. So the coward suppressed his anger and grinned at the boy's folly."

Ali paused to watch Moustache turn his back on Gurdit and walk toward the gangway. "The boy," he continued, "eventually became bored and was about to leave when the guard, noticing that everyone had disappeared and, seizing the opportunity, grabbed the boy by the back of the neck, thrust him against the rail, and lifted his arm to give the boy a slap." At that moment we all turned to Ali with the fierce and fiery eyes of men ready for action, for in our minds we imagined a stranger about to abuse our child. Then we turned to the immigration officers and we watched Moustache and his men board their launch.

A great anger surged within all of us. Ali continued with emotion, "But before he could let his hand fall, that passenger, the one with the mouth, the one who drags boats with his teeth, came out of nowhere, grabbed the hand, and yelled, 'No!'" Sunny held his hand out, imagining that he was holding the guard's hand, and Ali repeated, "No!" And then we all muttered the word under our breath. Ali continued, "Possibly the only word he knew in their language. He crushed the hand so that the paleface let go of the boy and fell to his knees, squirming and screaming for him to let go."

Sunny went though the actions, we regarded him for a moment, and then Ali went on. "The boy," he said, "ran off and returned with a procession of passengers ready to release days of accumulated anger and frustration upon him; but the passenger who had crushed his hand stopped them, and it was a good thing he did. That paleface would have been fish food." Then Sanjay corrected, "You mean 'Hindu' food." At the comment I stared quizzically at him; I asked him what he meant by such a foul comment, and he explained that Gurdit had read them an article the day before that assured all the good people of Vancouver that all Hindus were cannibals, and that if they let us disembark, they would have to keep a close eye on us and their poor children.

None of us laughed at the absurdity of the article; we knew it would help foster the environment of hate and fear the authorities needed to continue their abuse and with such things being written against us we'd never be allowed to disembark. I began to feel the anger again, and it drowned my soul in hatred for the man who had written those words. I wondered why he had written such lies and why he had consciously cho-sen to omit certain truths. Never once did their writers report that we were British subjects. Never once did they mention our loyalty to the King. Never once did they mention the illegal manoeuvres of the immi-gration officers. And now I see a change in the eyes around me: men, who had been taught all their lives to trust the newspapers, now view them with mingled suspicion and contempt, and we all knew that the writer of those words was just as responsible, if not more, for what was happening to us.

June 3

I learned some disturbing news about Hopkinson today. He claims to have significant influence over our individual cases. Apparently, our destinies have a price and that price is 9000 rupees. To whomever can afford this grotesque fee, he promises to somehow provide them with an opportunity to disembark.

Hopkinson is a man who should not be in a position of power, for power is a lion, and only those who understand the lion, who use the lion justly and fairly, who know how to tame the lion and use its strength sparingly, should be blessed with its presence. Hopkinson is not such a man. He has not earned the loyalty of the lion. Rather, he has snuck up on the beast, jumped on its back, grabbed it by its mane, and forced it to do his bidding. He has taken control of something that cannot be controlled, only understood. And now, through manipulation and trickery, he abuses the lion, forcing it to go against its nature. But how long, I wonder, can he hold on to that mane? How long can he abuse the lion to his end. How long before the lion thrusts him off its back and tears him to bits and pieces as it has done to so many men who have tried to control it without ever having taken the time to tame or understand it.

I watched Hopkinson walk around Nanak Jahaz. When he spotted the doctor, they signalled each other with their eyes, and Hopkinson quickly made his way up to the doctor's cabin. As I observed Hopkinson and the doctor discussing something rather heatedly, a passenger approached me. We watched them disapprovingly, and somehow we knew they were making plans against us. "He is corrupt," said the man, his eyes fixed on Hopkinson. I regarded the man a moment and then turned my gaze up to the upper housing. "The doctor?" I questioned.

The man shrugged. "Maybe," he said, "maybe the doctor is corrupt, but I mean the abuser, the one everyone talks about." I turned to the man. "Oh," I said, and then returned my gaze to Hopkinson. There was a short silence. The man broke the silence and said, "He has destroyed many lives." He sighed, shook his head, and went on. "He has never suffered a day in his life. That is why he cannot understand our suffering. Gurdit says he's taking bribes and that he will only help those who have the money to pay for it. But Gurdit has warned..." He stopped suddenly and his eyes seemed to laugh at the doctor. I questioned, "Warned?" He continued, "Hopkinson will steal every last rupee from you and then forget you ever existed, believing you're a no-good, uneducated farmer without the intelligence or means to take him to court. And if you do manage to take him to court, he knows no one will listen to your side of the story anyway. He knows that most judges have a great respect for the suit he wears and that they will believe anything he says. So, really, he has nothing to lose."

Another passenger joined us. He looked up at the doctor and Hopkinson, and seemed to know what they were discussing. He said wearily, "I hope that when he disembarks he finds a way to help us." The other passenger laughed, "Ha! The doctor? He'd throw us to the dogs to land! Why else do you think the immigration officers always want to talk to him?" He paused, we turned to him, and then he continued, "Because he'll say whatever they want him to say, sign whatever they want him to sign, do whatever they want him to do, just to…" But before he could finish his sentence, someone collapsed with a loud thud. We ran toward the frantic cries for help.

Not too far from where we were standing, we found the fallen man and surrounded him. The doctor rushed down from his cabin, but when he approached the sick man, a passenger pushed him away and commanded him to go back to Hopkinson. The doctor's eyes filled with fear. Now he knew how the passengers felt about him. I have never seen so much fear in a man's eyes. As the doctor stood, scared and startled by what had just happened, realizing no one on the ship trusted him anymore, one of the crewmen ran to us with water and poured it into the sick man's mouth. The water sputtered and splattered. The man coughed and tried his very best to speak, but couldn't for dryness and dehydration. A passenger turned to Hopkinson and yelled, "Water! We need water!" Then, realizing Hopkinson didn't understand Punjabi, he yelled in English, "Water! Water! Water, now!" To which Hopkinson grinned, seeming to enjoy his authority over us.

At night we slept on deck for the air was dank and heavy. All around Nanak Jahaz there were whispered stories of Hopkinson, some exaggerated and some not, but all were better than the silence that had plagued us for the last few days. Sanjay told us a funny story that he had heard from another passenger. "They say," he began with a little laugh, "that when he goes undercover, he wraps a turban around his head and sits in a Gurdwara and tries to mingle with the Sikhs."

We all laughed at the thought, and he repeated, "Mingle!" Ali lifted his hand to get our attention. "Yes!" said Ali, "Mingle! Mingle like a fox in a chicken coop!" We laughed at the things Hopkinson would do to justify his job and hold on to that mane. Then we stopped talking and laughing altogether, for the dryness in our throats was unbearably painful. And the silence was on us again.

Now I have nothing more to report except that I miss you dearly. Soon I will close my eyes and prepare to meet you in my dreams. I hope all is well with you, and I hope and pray that, if the news of our situation has reached your ears, the lies have not affected your opinion of me. One day you will be old enough to read this journal and understand.

June 4

Most passengers lie weak and helpless on the deck. The ship becomes filthier and filthier as the hours go by, for none of us have the will or energy to keep it clean. The stench is unbearable and I can't remember the last day any of us had food or water. Food we can do without for a little while, but not water. Today I tried to eat a piece of biscuit but, lacking moisture and saliva, it turned to dust in my mouth and I had to cough it out, for my dry and narrow throat would not allow the nourishment to fall.

Gurdit and the passengers committee have some provisions, but not much, just enough to keep their minds focused on finding a way to help us through this. I saw Gurdit attempt to give some of his food to a sick passenger. The passenger, with all the energy he had left, refused to take even a crumb of his beloved leader's food. I have never seen such loyalty. Gurdit promised us that we would all have food and water by the end of the day, and as he worked hard to help us, arguing and yelling with the immigration officers, the doctor worked even harder to steal power from Gurdit by spreading vile rumours about him and suggesting we lock Gurdit in his cabin and let him take over as leader of Nanak

Jahaz. No one listens to the doctor. He has done nothing for us. We know he has some sort of arrangement with Hopkinson, and that he wishes for what he does not understand.

Later in the day Gurdit, escorted by three or four immigration officers, boarded a launch that carried him to another launch where his lawyer stood leaning over the bow. They weren't permitted a private meeting--again violating our rights!--and the two of them had to remain on their respective launches to shout and discuss their plans while surrounded by a horde of immigration officers. I may not know much about law, but I do know a British subject is entitled to a private meeting with his legal representative. But because they have dragged this out so long, and have starved us like beasts, we accept this injustice without complaint, and are almost overjoyed with any crumb of justice they might throw our way. This is the way they work.

When Gurdit returned he was furious to the point of silence. As he stormed toward his cabin, he told us that he would let us know how things went in the morning and that he needed some time to think. But he did assure us that we would have food and water tomorrow and that we had local Indians in Vancouver helping us. He refers to them as the shore committee. They are determined to help us and stick by us to the very conclusion of this ordeal.

What a wonderful feeling it is to know that you are not alone, to know that others care about your huger and thirst, your pain and suffering. What a divine feeling it is to know that, in a world infected by self-interest and indifference, there are still those who are concerned about things like truth, rights, and justice; that there are those who cannot be spoiled, or convinced to look the other way simply because the tyrant dangles riches in front of them. What a divine feeling it is, indeed, to know that there are those who take the gifts Waheguru has bestowed upon them and use those gifts for the betterment of humanity; that they take their good fortune and spread it around rather than hoarding it like so many fear-stricken men I know. I have been told countless times that Waheguru only spoils those who cannot be spoiled, and these men and women who make up the shore committee, though strangers to me, will forever live in my heart. Now I know, despite the efforts of the newspapers and the writers who would write anything just to be published,

Waheguru has not abandoned Vancouver. I may be weak for hunger and dehydration, but my courage and strength are rekindled for strangers who refused to look the other way.

June 5

The cold wind screamed all around us, and every face looked as if it had aged a thousand years. In the early morning, Gurdit shouted over the wind what he had learned yesterday. Many of us were too weak to stand, so the strong supported the weak, the weak supported the weaker, and we all tried our best to keep our minds off of our hunger and thirst. We focused on his words, which were severe, disturbing, and demoralizing. Apparently, the immigration officers will resort to anything to force us home. In a most illegal and immoral attempt to prevent Gurdit from paying the final instalment of the charter, they are now preventing him from unloading and selling the coal he had taken on in Japan. He went on to explain that the owner of the ship would force the captain to return to Japan if he did not honour the contract. Having nothing else to tell us, Gurdit put his head down in shame. Our hearts sank with his.

His boy edged closer to him and took his hand. Gurdit looked to his son and took strength from him; his head snapped up and he continued. He said the immigration officers had won because they were willing to do what we weren't: defy the King and break the laws. When one man suggested we take over the ship so the captain couldn't force us back home, Gurdit shook his head and said he refused to turn abuser simply because he had been abused. He said sharply, "The captain is a good man. I will not abuse him or make him or his men suffer because we are being abused, because we are being made to suffer. Or else, really, we are no better than them."

No one disagreed, but a passenger yelled, "Then let us stay until we are forced home!" Another yelled, "Those cowards haven't done half the things I've done for the King and they presume! they presume! to treat me like this! No, I'd rather die than be treated like this." Suddenly a great roar came from the passengers. The man continued, "Bhai Gurditji, please! Before I go home, before my son is sent away to fight and die for

this King, I want to know: Am I a dog of the Empire, or am I a subject?"
And there came another great roar, and those who could not use their
throats stamped their feet. Gurdit nodded his understanding and then
silenced everyone with a wave of his hand. "We will stay," he said, and
turned to the captain, who was watching us from the housing above. He
turned back to us and said, "At least until the captain is commanded to
take us back home." Gurdit flicked his eyes to the doctor. He looked deep
into his eyes, while he warned us there were traitors among us. As he
spoke, he watched the doctor's eyes, and he watched how they involun-
tarily sought out the men with whom he was conspiring.

June 6

Thanks to the shore committee, fresh water was pumped on board and
two weeks worth of flour, oil, and lentils were hauled below deck into the
communal kitchen. We ate our first real meal since we arrived and
received the water as if it were amrita. I only drank half a glass, but I
savoured each and every drop; it must have taken me the entire day to
finish what had been given to me. When every drop had been consumed,
I looked up to the heavens and thanked Waheguru for the blessing. Now,
with rekindled strength, Sanjay and Ali are back at their games. Battling
despair with laughter, they spent the entire day with a group of passengers playing their imaginary conversation game. Sunny is also much
stronger; he seems to be accepting the situation rather than allowing
himself to be defeated by it.
    When night set its dark shell over us, the wind howled and it
began to rain fat drops so we, despite the violent wind, actually bathed
outside under a communal shower. I must admit many of us were hysteri-
cal in the water. Some even wiggled around in puddles and almost
drowned in them! As we enjoyed the heavenly shower, Gurdit and the
passengers committee found every empty receptacle there was on Nanak
Jahaz and left them on deck to fill with fresh water. Afterward, despite
the thick and heavy air below, many of us descended to the kitchen and
huddled around a small cooking fire. With the rain pattering outside like
a million ants on the march, Sunny told us a story, the first since we had

arrived. With the fire shadows leaping on his face, he began strongly, "In Calcutta there is the story of the mother who gave her life for her boy." He immediately had our attention and everyone fell quiet. Beads of rain glistened and dripped from his beard. He shifted under his blanket as his eyes searched inward for the story. He continued softly, "She was a poor woman who cleaned homes for food. Every day she cleaned the home of a rich merchant who lived many miles from her home. Every morning she brought her boy to help her, and every afternoon they walked home together, talking about the things a mother and son talk about, while carrying the food they had earned. One day, following their usual path by the forest, talking about the feast they would later prepare for dinner, a tiger leapt into the clearing." He stopped suddenly. His gaze swept over us, and he saw with pleasure the reality of this place melting away.

When he saw his story glowing in all of our eyes, he continued, "Before the mother could hide her boy behind her, the tiger pounced on him and bit into his leg. The mother, without hesitation, without thinking about her own life, attacked the tiger. She kicked the tiger, then leapt onto the beast and wrestled and fought with it. The tiger released her boy to take care of the immediate threat on its back. But there was something in the mother that was greater than the tiger; greater than any tiger. There was something that the tiger had not counted on." He stopped and gazed at each of us with an intense seriousness on his face. I swallowed my breath. Sanjay swallowed his breath. Ali demanded he continue. Sunny squinted, lifted his finger, and continued, "And that something was the strength and determination of a mother's love. It was the realization that if the tiger defeated her, her son would be next." He put his finger down and his hands began to fight with something only he could see. "So the mother fought the tiger with an unparalleled fury, a fury unknown to man or beast, and she overcame the tiger and killed it. To this very day no one knows how she did it. And without any weapons!"

He lifted his arms to show us his bare hands, pausing to give us a chance to imagine the words he had just spoken; then he continued, "Badly cut everywhere, bleeding profusely, and on the verge of death, she lifted her injured boy and carried him for hours under a scorching sun, leaving a bloody trail behind her. Some say other tigers smelled the blood and came out into the clearing, but when they saw the mother with the

limp boy in her arms, they turned around and returned to the forest."
Then Sunny paused, and because he had not explained why the tigers
would not attack the mother and her boy, we all searched inward for our
own reasons. When Sunny felt we had each found the reason he had
wanted us to seek, he continued, "Shivering with pain, she forced herself
to the doctor's home and gently placed her boy at his doorstep. She
knocked on the door with the last of her strength, then collapsed and died
with her arms around her boy." A hush fell over us as the story left everyone searching deep within themselves for the strength and courage it
would take to defeat a tiger. We all saw ourselves as the mother, and each
of us knew that we would do the same. Slowly, his story reinforced our
strength and resolve to defeat the tiger in our path.

A passenger lying close by overheard the story and turned to
Sunny to ask him if it were true. When Sunny nodded, the man asked if
he could retell it to some of his friends whom he thought could use such
a story. Sunny smiled and nodded. He went over to the man and told
another group the story. Only this time Sunny completely lost himself in
the telling of the tale. His eyes grew fierce with the descriptions and he
moved around and made fantastic sound effects with his mouth. When he
spoke of danger, his eyes went wide with fear; and when he spoke of the
fight, he punched the air as if he were struggling with the beast. His elaborate movements attracted men from all over the ship, and, each time a
new man came, he was asked to retell the tale. And each time he did, he
told a slightly different story, but never once did he lose his energy or
enthusiasm. It was as though he fed off of the immense pleasure he was
giving these men, who just a moment ago seemed empty and lifeless.

Later that night, when the passengers slept and dreamt of the tiger
they each would battle for their children, Amar, drenched in sweat, woke
in a panic and made for the outside, regardless of the storm, which
refused to subside. He spent the whole night pacing the deck, mumbling
and apologizing to some mysterious apparition only he could see. When I
went up to see if he was okay, I hid behind a lifeboat and watched him
stumble over his words, when, to my horror, he fell to his knees, threw
his hands together in prayer, and begged Waheguru for forgiveness.

June 7

Nothing today. Some of us still stare at the shore from time to time with a lingering hope. Others despair and think negative thoughts all day; thereby allowing themselves to wallow in their misery and be destroyed by negative thoughts. The ship is a mess and few passengers pick up after themselves. I feel the filth is affecting us all in a deep, demoralizing way. It's hard to even believe that this is the same ship we arrived on. At least Sunny is himself again.

June 8

A few passengers prepared their bags in the evening. Their faces didn't display even the slightest degree of happiness. I suppose they could afford Hopkinson's fee. Many of us stared at them with contempt. Some of us even approached them and made them promise they wouldn't forget us when they disembarked. But we know they won't. We also know it is to our advantage to have them on shore where they can join the shore committee and help us all see justice.

June 9

Under a clear sky filled with birds, twenty or so passengers, some with their heads down, some looking at us with promising eyes, walked across the gangplank and onto a launch that would ferry them to the pier where the actors had begun their performance again. The children and the two women were the first people allowed to board, but when Gurdit attempted to convince his boy to leave with the others, the boy told his father he was old enough to stay and he refused to leave his father in this time of great need. And so, Gurdit's boy is now the only child left on Nanak Jahaz.

　　　As the launch began to plough through the water, one of the passengers called out to them, "Don't forget us!" Another passenger took off a sandal and waved it angrily at Hopkinson. Our eyes followed after them until they were landed and a group of local Indians took their bags and helped them keep their balance. The actors screamed and roared their ugly song, they gave the reporters a show that would sell more papers and keep public opinion exactly where they wanted it. Hopkinson wanted to bring the doctor ashore, but the passengers would only allow his family to go, for we feel the doctor has been a traitor since the beginning and that he is a big part of the reason why we are having so much trouble finding justice. Whether he likes it or not, for having betrayed us, he will suffer with us.

June 10

A thick fog hung over us all day and no one did anything. Everyone lay around the ship staring inwards, thinking about home, despairing. I was nostalgic all day. Nothing is familiar or kind about this place. I miss my village. I miss my family. I miss you!

June 11

We have food and water, but we lack hope. Today was Gurdit's last chance to pay the final instalment but the anarchists made sure this would never happen. To prevent Gurdit from selling his coal; to have him break a promise to a client for no reason, no reason at all, is a measure of how far Moustache and Hopkinson will go to keep us out of Canada.

Waheguru, help me understand why this is happening to us and our families. What are we supposed to learn from this? Many of us would rather die than return home in shame, for there is no greater shame than the shame of a father who has failed his family.

June 12

The oppressed can overcome anything if they stick together. The shore
committee, much to Hopkinson's disapproval, held a meeting in an
empty, run-down hall last night where many men spoke to the local
Indians about our plight, our troubles, and how we, soldiers of the
Empire, farmers of the Empire, lions of the Empire, were being treated
like dogs by corrupt officials, who would break any law, blurt any lie,
and forge any document to keep the "Hindu Invaders" from landing. The
men spoke vehemently and the crowd roared their anger, but when there
was a call for pledges, a deathly silence fell over the people. Their heads
fell, for they missed their families immensely and every dollar they saved
was a day closer to home. These men, who have been treated like scum,
these men who have been deposited in the slums of Vancouver and forced
to live in abandoned factories without heat or electricity, who stuck
together, worked together, and lived together to overcome a racist and
fear-stricken Vancouver, these men lowered their heads in despair for
they knew they couldn't allow Nanak Jahaz to crawl back home defeated
by the corrupt officials who, for the last decade, had rendered them invisible to the good people of Vancouver. And yet, how they missed their
wives, their children, their friends! How they missed them all, and how
they wished to finally end the separation.

    Conflicted men held their heads down. After a moment, a young
man stood from his seat with great difficulty. Heads began to rise. The
young man lifted himself, holding onto self-made crutches. He struggled
and shook under the strain, braced himself and, placing one crutch in
front of the other, slowly made his way to the leaders of the shore committee. Eyes followed him to the front. Once there he leaned one of his
crutches on the table and unravelled his turban. When his turban was
loose enough to slip his hand underneath, he retrieved a bundle of
money--his savings, all of his savings--and put it on the table. He turned
and gazed triumphantly at Hopkinson, who had been sent to supervise
and translate the speeches. Hopkinson looked into his eyes, seeming to
see the man for the first time. The man returned to his seat and as he sat,
two other men stood and made their way to the front of the room. By the
end of the night, an invisible community suddenly appeared before

Hopkinson and showed him that they were not going to let others be treated as they had been treated for the last decade, even if it cost them years more of separation. A mountain of money, pledges, and real estate titles stood before Hopkinson. He watched men add to that mountain the whole night long. Many said that Hopkinson was entranced by the money and that, if he could have gotten away with it, he would have slaughtered everyone and run away with the money. I suppose we are treating Hopkinson as the newspapers are treating us. I guess we also need a monster.

The war isn't over, but this battle is won! We have beaten Hopkinson and Moustache. The final instalment was paid and Gurdit says, with pride, that we now have enough money to stay here for the next year or two if need be, and that he will now demand that each and every one of us get a proper hearing as we should have gotten when we first arrived. Tonight I fall asleep with the goodness of those strangers in my heart, those strangers who sacrificed everything in the name of truth and justice. As I gaze up at the stars, I see that man with the crutches walking up to the front of the room, unravelling his turban, and handing over his life savings. I see the bundle fall on the table and I see Hopkinson's eyes grow wide, knowing he would never do such a thing for a fellow man. Now Moustache and Hopkinson know it will take a lot more malicious, bureaucratic footwork to make Nanak Jahaz crawl back home.

I wonder if I would have done the same. We've been separated for only a few months and already the separation is unbearable. But I'm sure I would have and I'm sure one day Waheguru will put my soul to the test. Maybe this is it. Maybe this is our test. Will the situation define us or will we define the situation? Will we let our heads sink and allow ourselves to be defeated, or will we raise our chins, meet the oppressor square in the eye, and demand our rights? Will we feel sorry for ourselves and let negative thoughts drag us into hell, or will we keep our eyes open for all that is good and divine, and search for the lesson in this? Well, my son, I couldn't call myself your father if I'd let this situation define me. I am positive, and I still see the good in all. I am trying my best to understand why we must go through this. There is a reason; there always is.

June 16

Garbage everywhere and I'm starting to feel like most of us are letting
this situation defeat us. No one makes the effort to keep things clean. It's
demoralizing. It's so dirty that you have to watch every step for fear of
stepping in filth.

June 17

This morning a few passengers had an argument with the doctor. They
don't want him talking to Hopkinson anymore. Their anger escalated and
they were soon pushing him across the upper deck. The doctor made
derogatory comments about them being simple farmers, and a few of
those "simple" farmers lifted the doctor over their heads and prepared to
throw him overboard. Luckily, Gurdit saw what was taking place. He ran
down from his cabin and stopped them just before they did something
they would regret. The passengers shouted angrily and said they didn't
want the doctor talking to the officials anymore. Gurdit suggested imprisoning him in his cabin instead of throwing him overboard. So now the
doctor is in his room, with a guard by his door.

In the evening, Gurdit warned us that this would be our last meal
until the shore committee could raise some more money for provisions.
He then began to summarize his progress with the immigration officials.
Things aren't very hopeful. They refuse to let anyone appear in court and,
as always, refuse to commit to any reason why. Gurdit said he will write
to the King.

June 18

They are trying to starve us home. This is the measure of their justice.
These are their tactics. This is why they won't give us a court date. Gurdit
said they had stopped the shore committee from sending us supplies and
will only let them provision Nanak Jahaz when we are ready to leave.
They are desperate. They don't have the cooperation of the Japanese crew

61

and their only spy is being held captive in his room.

June 19

Everyone is irritable. We've been here too long. The filth is playing on the mood of the ship. Malnutrition and sickness are eating away at our patience and dignity. I can no longer think of us as individuals. We are so in-tune with one another that our moods and temperaments are the same. Our suffering is the same. Our struggle is the same. We are one. We are Nanak Jahaz, and as Nanak Jahaz we are struggling against a great oppressor, and it is hard, if not impossible, to win any battle when you are hungry and weak. But I suppose the immigration officers know this.

At night, just before the moon rose, Amar nearly killed Sunny. It happened like this. Amar had been gazing at his certificate all day when Sunny, frustrated and irritated with our situation, turned on Amar and fired off an unusual comment. "You know what I bet?" he said, staring first at the certificate, then into Amar's eyes. "I bet that if I were to take that certificate--that certificate of honour--and if I were to twist it, I bet blood would drip out." There was a long silence. Amar stared at Sunny with eyes that began to water. I put my arm on Sunny's shoulder as if to stop him from uttering another word. Then I said, "Leave it be." He thrust his shoulder away from me and said, "No! I will not leave it be. All he does is make everyone uncomfortable. He sits there with that paper and thinks he's done the world a great deed. And when he's not admiring his courage, he's judging us with his looks. His eyes. His judging eyes. Now it's my turn to take the role of judge." Amar's eyes widened on Sunny. "Right?" continued Sunny, "I bet if I were to take that certificate and wring it, blood would pour out by the glass!" With his hands he pre-tended to wring the certificate. Then he looked to the floor and pointed to the imaginary blood. "Look," he said, staring at the floor, "Sikh blood! Hindu blood! Muslim blood! Indian blood!" A tear slipped down Amar's cheek, and slowly lost itself in the thick of his beard. His eyes were red; his breathing, heavy. Ali and Sanjay said in unison, "Okay, Sunny, it's enough." But before any of us could say another word, Amar had Sunny by the throat. Amar squeezed and squeezed as we pleaded for him to

62

stop.

     Sunny looked his aggressor straight in the eye and challenged him to end his life. He struggled to say death was nothing to him and he welcomed it as he welcomed Waheguru. Then, as suddenly as he had attacked him, Amar released him, regarded him for a moment, and stormed away. Sunny coughed and struggled for breath as Sanjay and Ali rushed to help him. I rose to my feet and followed Amar. I followed him to the other side of the ship where, standing by the rail, he motioned me away. When I refused to listen and continued to approach him, he turned on me with death in his eyes and commanded me to leave him alone. Hearing the gravity in his tone, and counter to my better judgement, I left him alone, again.

June 20

All around Nanak Jahaz tempers are flaring, and Amar has isolated himself from everyone. Sunny made a move to apologize but Amar yelled for him to leave him alone. I am worried for him. No man should be alone for too long, for such solitude, though good in moderation, can change a man for the worse. He may learn to rely on himself and himself only and such knowledge would cripple his soul. For it is a blessing to need others, to rely on others, to share and grow with others, to learn and experience with others. A man who no longer needs others is hardly a man. A man who no longer needs others is fallen and needs someone to pull him out of his solitude and show him the innate goodness of people and the divine gift that is friendship.

June 21

Nanak Jahaz seems to be falling apart, and so Gurdit herded all passengers on deck to demonstrate something his father used to show him, and my father showed me for that matter. He came down from his cabin holding a bundle of sticks. We gathered around round him. He didn't utter a word. He simply placed the bundle on the ground, pulled out a stick,

63

and held it up to everyone. He paused and then snapped it in two. He then picked up another stick and repeated the process. He continued to do this until he had broken about five or six sticks. Then, without uttering a word, he held the bundle out to us and tried to break all the sticks at once. He struggled with the bundle and hardly bent it. He laughed at the strength of the bundle and then handed it over to a passenger to help him. The passenger tried his best, but failed with every attempt. The passenger passed on the bundle and many passengers endeavoured to break it with the same result. Eventually, the bundle made its way into the hands of the passenger who had dragged the boat with his mouth. The man held it up and we all waited in anticipation. He went to break the bundle, but, red in the face, he too hardly bent it. A few passengers tried to help him, but still they could not break it. Then Gurdit walked up to him, took the bundle back, held it high in the air, and said, "Continue fighting amongst yourselves and the tyrant will snap us one at a time like a twig. Stick together, work together, and that very same tyrant won't even bend us!" Then, having conveyed the message he wanted to convey, he made his way to his cabin while his son remained on deck, trying, without success, to bend the bundle.

June 22

We ran out of water today. We haven't much time now and must pray that the anarchists find it within their hearts to let the provisions through. Sadly, Gurdit told us this was highly unlikely and they would only let the provisions through if we agreed to leave. Then he told us that they won't give us access to the courts, that none of us will get a hearing, and that Moustache is purposely avoiding our lawyer because he knows he is breaking the law.

June 23

Somehow, through the despair and hopelessness, Ali and Sanjay have found another way to keep their minds off of things. We were lying on deck when a seagull perched on a lifeboat. Our stomachs empty and begging for food, we all stared at the bird with the same thought. No one said a word, we just watched the bird. It must have sensed our hunger, for as soon as it turned toward us, it screamed for its life and took to the sky. Our eyes followed the bird until it disappeared from sight. After a moment Ali said, "Who knows when they'll let provisions through." Sanjay, as if reading his thoughts, said, "You can't catch a bird!" Ali responded defensively, "I've caught chickens." Sanjay laughed, "Chickens can't fly!" To which Ali asserted, "Chickens are fast!" Sanjay laughed aloud. He shook his head and said, "A dead turtle would have a better chance." Ali squinted. He pointed to his chest and said, "Are you saying I'm slow? Is that what you're saying!" Sanjay answered, "No, I'm saying a dead turtle would have a better chance." At which point Sunny blurted out, "Hey brothers, bundle of sticks, remember?" Sanjay and Ali regarded Sunny and fell silent.

They stared at the sky, watching a bird circle Nanak Jahaz. Suddenly, Ali broke the silence and said, "What would you do if I caught one?" Sanjay said teasingly, "I'd eat it, that's what! And then I'd wash your clothes for all eternity. In fact, I'd make it so that my children wash your children's clothes and their children wash their children's clothes…" Ali raised a serious finger at Sanjay, then pointed at Sunny and me. Finally he said, "They are my witnesses." Sanjay gasped and said, "How foolish! You're not going to catch a bird!" But Ali was serious. He stood and searched the deck for a bird, and all day he chased and leapt and cornered seagulls that were too cunning to be caught. When the sun dropped and plunged us into darkness, Ali gave up the hunt and returned to his spot. Sanjay was too weak to chide him.

Later that night Amar came to me and put a leather purse in my hands. He whispered for me to share its contents with Sunny, and then he disappeared. When I opened the purse, I was shocked to find all of his money. I stared at the money and something dark stirred inside me. I leapt to my feet and knew I had to find him.

June 24

I spent all of last night searching for Amar. I searched the latrines, the cabins, the kitchen, the engine room. I even scanned the sleeping faces, one by one, hoping to see his rigid face among them. But he was nowhere to be found.

In the afternoon Gurdit made an announcement. He explained that he had made a deal with the immigration officers yesterday. He told them that we would leave as soon as they signed a document explaining why we were refused entry and legal representation. He went on to say that we would use this letter to sue the Crown as soon as we got back home.

Apparently Moustache laughed, said it would be his pleasure, and that he would bring the letter today. Gurdit says we should be ready to leave anytime, but none of us were pleased about this. Some grunted their disapproval, seeing it as a lack of courage on our part. Others shouted that we had done nothing wrong and shouldn't have to crawl back home like cowards. And some even swore they would take a lifeboat and make for shore if they had to return to debt, hunger, and overbearing taxes. Gurdit explained that these people can't see the humanity in us and will, without a second thought, let us die out here. Moreover, he said that as long as they admitted to denying each of us an opportunity to appear before a board of inquiry we would find redress in India.

I fear Gurdit may be right. Many of us are on the verge of death, the doctor is locked up, and the ship is so dirty there is hardly room to move. I look around me and feel that we are slowly becoming the beasts they are treating us like. Waheguru, stay with us.

In the evening we discovered that Moustache refused to give Gurdit the letter. I suppose Moustache decided it wasn't such a good idea after all. I suppose deep down he realizes he is breaking many laws. Deep down he knows our lawsuit would be successful, and that he would most likely lose his job; so now, they've cleverly come up with their own proposal. They say that if we agree to one test case they will provision Nanak Jahaz. One test case to represent three hundred and fifty men! Imagine! But Gurdit says this is probably our best chance, especially if they won't give us that letter; besides, we really need water. Gurdit was optimistic about the test case. He said we might even have a chance and if they adhere to the law, it won't matter who represents us for they'll have no choice but to let us disembark. Then one man said they hadn't followed the law since we got here and we shouldn't assume they'll start now. I agree with that passenger, but I also agree with Gurdit: we need water!

June 25

They provisioned Nanak Jahaz for a few days, and chose a man named Munshi Singh to represent us. He is already gone, and the hearing will most likely take place today. I never realized how fast and easy it was to see a judge in this place. Gurdit paced Nanak Jahaz at a rapid stride the entire day, worrying about Munshi, worrying about our futures. The captain paced with him.

June 26

There is no justice in a country where the prosecutors are the judges. Munshi returned a defeated man. With Gurdit by his side, he explained to us what had taken place. He said that he had told the Board that he had come from a small village in India, leaving a wife and daughter. He told them that he had had no harvest for two years and that he had heard fantastic rumours about a part of the Empire where they were practically giving out good land for farmers to use and develop. He said that a soldier had brought a handbill to his village that he had acquired from his travels in Europe. The handbill was basically asking for farmers from the European continent to immigrate to Canada with promises of free land and all sorts of other incentives. He then said that he did what any father in his situation would have done: he sought a way to get some land for his family. So he set out to purchase a ticket on a steam liner, but no company would sell him a ticket to Canada. That's when he heard about Gurdit's mission. His mission to bring his people to this land. And so he bought a ticket for Hong Kong, where Gurdit had begun the journey, but when he arrived he was too late; Nanak Jahaz had already left. So, having being told by men at the Gurdwara that Nanak Jahaz was to stop in Shanghai and Yokohama, he purchased a ticket for Yokohama and caught up with Gurdit there.

He then told the Board that he was a farmer with many acres of land in Punjab, land which was ready to be sold as soon as he established himself in Canada. But the Board concluded that he had no proof of owning such land, or of being a farmer, and that until he could furnish such proof he would not be admitted. Then Munshi told us that he had lost his composure and had demanded to know why farmers with no ties to the Crown were being given land when he, a loyal subject, was being treated like an alien. Why were white aliens being lured to Canada while brown subjects were being rejected? They ignored him and passed a judgement that had already been determined long before the hearing had begun. Now our lawyer is appealing their order to deport Nanak Jahaz and we should have our answer in a week or so. Gurdit then took over and said that he had heard about a plan to steal a lifeboat and head for shore. He pleaded that the men planning to do this reconsider. He said that to do such a thing was to betray Nanak Jahaz, and he said that to do such a thing was to reduce oneself to a criminal in a situation where the only criminals were the officials. He asked that we stay true to the Crown.

I have a difficult time understanding the officials of this country. I don't understand the way their minds work. This is a country where bureaucratic walls are raised against the Asian and every law is set up for the European. But this will only make Asians stronger, smarter, and much, much faster! These anarchists think they will strengthen their kind by making things easy for their children and difficult for ours; but the only thing they will succeed at doing is making our children more hardworking, more dedicated, and more determined so that in a hundred years the man who cuts the trees will own the lumberyard. So that in a hundred years their children will serve our children.

By constantly challenging our children and making things difficult for them, they will keep their minds alert and ready for any circumstance while their children's minds, protected and secure in their laws, will putrefy like stagnant water. Of this I am certain, for it is not a question of skin colour or race, but rather of scarcity and abundance and the survival instincts the former develops and the latter diminishes. Their children will have everything given to them and our children will have to fight for everything, and that will be the difference. The whole difference.

Their children will grow lazy and slow in their security while ours will grow strong and cunning; and when our children tear down the walls of injustice, their children will have as much a chance at surviving as llamas thrown to the lions. These anarchists established laws to keep their children rich and powerful, but, in reality, all they have done is ensure their extinction. A hundred years from now the Asians will dominate this cold, unfriendly place. The Asians will own all the homes and farms and businesses; and the slums where they currently live, where they've been swept into, hidden, and forgotten like dirt under a rug, will be overflowing with the children of their oppressors. But it is my hope that our children will be more benevolent and understanding; and will, in the very least, treat their children as men, not beasts. It is my hope that our oppressed children will not turn into oppressors themselves, as is often the case with the oppressed. For, if they do, the cycle will continue and the Asians, in their abundance, will soon return to the slums.

June 27

We have food and water! There is no experience that equals the first sip of water after days without. There is nothing more valuable. I wouldn't trade a glass, a sip, a drop for a sea of gold! So abundant, so pure, so taken for granted is water. So important a thing that three or four days without and death is imminent. So simple. So transparent. And yet, so deceptive, for in its heart lies the key to life and the history of the world.

The entire evening I searched the decks for Amar with no luck. I looked everywhere. When I finally gave up and took my place beside Sunny, Sunny turned to me, tapped me on the shoulder and asked if I had seen him. I said I hadn't, and he sighed heavily. "Do you think he's all right?" he asked me in a whisper. I looked at him and sensed his regret. "I'm not sure," I answered. He crossed his hands and looked at the stars and said, "I didn't mean what I said." He glanced at me. I said, "I know you didn't." "Where do you suppose he is?" he asked. I shrugged after a heavy silence. He said, "I hope he's okay." He sighed, and I added, "Me too."

We tried to sleep but with little success, as too much was going through our minds. In the middle of the night Sunny turned to me again and asked, "You awake?" I answered, "I am." His eyes lifted to the clear night sky. "Sure is a beautiful night," he observed, and I agreed. "It is," I said. He looked back at me. "You think of home?" he asked. "All the time," was my reply. There was a long silence. Then Sunny broke the silence, saying, "My wife and I could spend the whole night gazing at a sky like this...and my son loved nights like this. Oh, he would take her hand and try to..." He stopped, for his voice had begun to tremble and he could feel the emotion climbing in his throat. I watched him in silence and then confided, "My wife would sing on a night like this! For no reason at all. Just sing." He laughed at the thought and forgot his despair. "She has such a beautiful voice," I continued about your mother, "you'd think she was an angel." Then Sunny beamed at me. His smile grew bigger and bigger, and I asked, "What!"

He squinted, and now his cheeks were touching his ears. "Is that who you write to?" he asked, poking me teasingly, as if I had committed some misdeed. I was surprised. I thought I had kept my journal writing sessions a secret. I feigned ignorance. "What do you mean?" I asked. He laughed. "Come on!" he said, "I see you waiting for us to sleep. I see you waiting, waiting to pull that book out of your jacket and do your scribbling!" He poked me again and asked, "Are you writing her poems?" I smiled at the thought; he laughed and continued, "If I could write, I'd write my wife some real nice poems. Oh, I would! Real nice and meaningful poems!" Then he observed the sky and repeated dreamily, "If I could write, I'd write her a poem."

There was a short silence, and then Sunny observed, "It's funny. Back home, seeing her every day, I wouldn't have even considered writing a poem or doing anything like that. Now, separated, I'd...I'd...well, I'd write her volumes." He paused thoughtfully, then added, "It's funny how things are, isn't it? How some situations make you think of things you would have never otherwise considered." I nodded my agreement, and, after a moment, I confessed, "Actually, I'm writing to my son." His eyes went wide. "Your son!" he exclaimed. I nodded and continued, "He's more stubborn than his mother! I left and he couldn't understand

70

why…he couldn't understand why I had to go. Wouldn't say good-bye, refused to even look at me, you know. Almost destroyed me inside. But my wife had an idea and she said that this would be kind of like bringing him with me." Sunny nodded his understanding and whispered, "I wish I could write." He paused and closed his eyes to form a picture of his son in his mind. After a moment, he opened his eyes and declared, "My son will know how to write. He will know how to write and he will know the books. No matter what. Whatever it takes, I will make sure he learns." Then he gazed back at the sky, shook his head slowly, and promised himself, "He will not be like me."

The night progressed and, still, we couldn't sleep. Sunny turned to me, knowing I was still awake, and asked, "Do you write about me?" When I didn't answer, a radiant smile grew on his face; he pointed at me and said, "You do! I knew it! What do you say?" The events of the journey quickly sprang into his mind. He said, "Did you write about how I jumped overboard and pulled you out of the water…how I saved you from certain death?" I raised my eyebrows at him and questioned, "You jumped overboard? I fell in the water?" His face grew serious and he said, "No…but it sounds a lot better than a group of terrified men formed a human chain and pulled you over the railing." I laughed and fell silent. I evaded his questioning eyes. He prodded me and demanded, "Come on, then, what did you say?" I turned to him, grinning. His eyes went wide in anticipation. "I think…" I said, placing a finger to my forehead, "I think I wrote something about…something…about how you were a good man." Sunny nodded, "Go on, I like that." I continued, "I wrote about how you treated everyone with respect." He agreed, "I do. Go on, that's good. I like that." I went on, "About how you always talk to yourself…" Sunny's head recoiled in disbelief, and he interrupted, "I don't talk to myself! Ahh! I don't like that! I don't like that at all! Don't write that…I just think things and say things aloud, but I in no way talk to myself."

I observed him with a serious face and said, "Sunny, you laugh at your own jokes, you ask yourself questions, you answer those questions…Sunny, brother, you talk to yourself." He pounced, "Yeah, but don't write that!" He seemed rather upset. He heaved a deep breath and then let it slip out slowly. It took a moment for him to accept my observations. Then he squinted and asked for more. He inquired, "What else?

What else do I do?" I smiled inwardly. "Well," I said, "you want to know what I wrote?" He nodded, "What?" I paused and like he had done so many times to us with his stories I made him wait until I saw in his eyes he could wait no more. When I saw his lips about to move, I said, "I wrote that you're a mood changer."

He nodded pensively and ran his fingers across his beard, wondering if that was a good thing. He wasn't sure, and so he asked, "Is that good or bad?" I answered carefully, "In some cases, good; in others, bad. In your case, good." He nodded his approval and said, "Good! That's good then." I continued without interruption, "I wrote that you can take any room and fill it with hope, life, and energy. That every night you go out of your way to tell us stories, really nice stories, stories that take us away from this place and transport us to incredible places, friendly and warm places, inspiring places...I wrote that you really go out of your way to show us everything that is good in people and, because you do, you make us feel good about ourselves, you change us in good ways."

Sunny was taken by my words. After a long reflective silence, he asked, "You really like my stories?" I assured him, "We all do." His eyes dropped a short moment, he considered his reasons, and then he looked up at me and said, "I never knew you guys liked my stories. I just say them because...well...because...I guess it's like you said, I get tired of everyone looking the way they do, and I just wish I could make them feel better..." He paused, thought for a moment, and then added, "I wish I could write." He fell silent. He looked at me long and hard and then suddenly thought of something. His eyes shone with a plan, and he said, "Maybe one day, when this is all over, we could write a story about what happened here. I could tell it and you could write it, and then everyone would know how they treated us." Then, as quickly as the thought entered his mind, disappointment washed over his face, and he fell silent again. He said despairingly, "But they wouldn't believe us. No, they wouldn't believe us. Not after all those things the newspapers said about us."

I began to twist and twirl my beard. "We trust the papers more than we should," I said pensively, thinking about all the horrible things the newspapers had said about us. Sunny promised, "Never again!" Then he turned to me and asked, "Why do you suppose they write those things?" I thought about the men who wrote those wicked words, and I felt my anger rising. When I didn't answer, Sunny added, "They're just as corrupt as those keeping us out." I disagreed. They were worse. I shook my head, opened my mouth, and suddenly rapid and intense words began to pour out:

"Worse! They keep the fires of hate and fear burning strong and fierce. Without their lies do you really believe they could get away with the way they're treating us? Without their lies, the people of Vancouver would be forced to think of us as human beings, and you don't starve and humiliate human beings like this. You don't. When they should be writing about our rights as British subjects, they are fabricating lies about the way we live. They call us invaders and cannibals. They pick and choose what they want to write. They're like artists creating a sculpture, only they're creating an opinion, and that opinion is a key, a key that will either open or close the heart…the key they've created for us, I'm afraid, bolts the heart against us."

For a long time Sunny thought about my words. Then he heaved a deep breath and said, "When the heart is closed, you cannot reason with a man." But I hardly heard him. I was still thinking about those who were responsible for creating the atmosphere of fear the immigration officers required to continue their abuse. "No," I said, "They are just as responsible, if not more, for what is happening to us." A silence swept over us, and the silence lasted for quite a while. Then Sunny pulled something out of his bag and held it in front of me. "Did I show you this?" he asked, holding out a carved piece of driftwood that resembled a dog. I examined it and asked him what it was. He said, "It's for my boy. He loves horses, so I thought I'd carve him one. Probably be finished by the time I see him again."

I looked at the wooden sculpture and questioned, "A horse?" He looked at it, observed it, tilted his head left, then right, then he turned the sculpture in the moonlight, and finally he turned to me with his mouth wide open. Having nothing to say, he closed his mouth and regarded his work again. He seemed a little disappointed. "Well," he said, "you'll see. Once I'm finished with it…it will be a horse." I smiled and said, "It will be whatever you want it to be." He laughed joyously, then became altogether serious. He gazed at me with an inquiring look and asked, "Will you write about tonight?" I felt for my inner pocket, felt my journal, and answered, "I will." He considered something very seriously; then he asked, "Can you write that I'm sorry about what I said to Amar?"

I placed my hand on his shoulder, felt his regret, and nodded, "I will." He shut his eyes and after a long while a soft snoring issued from his lips. I observed a soft moon in the sky. I stood and looked toward the pier and my eyes wandered to a building close by. From one of the windows light poured out and softly receded into the darkness. Gurdit had told us that this building was the immigration building, and that they had anchored us here to keep a close and constant eye on Nanak Jahaz.

June 28

Last night, as I finished writing and closed the journal, I saw a shadowy figure emerge from below deck and walk toward the bow. A wave of relief came over me, as I immediately recognized the rigid gait and the stern posture. I placed my journal back in my jacket and placed my jacket into my bag. Then I rose carefully and walked toward the bow and, quiet as the breeze whispering in my ears, I approached Amar from behind. This time I didn't ask him anything or disturb him. I merely stood beside him and stared at the stars in the water. He turned to me, regarded me for a moment, then turned back to the water and said, "Go away." But I didn't listen. After a short silence, I said, "Don't do it." To which he responded by lifting his hand and motioning me away. But I didn't listen. Instead I took a step closer and said softly, "Brother, whatever it is…" He interrupted me by throwing his hand in the air and saying in a harsh whisper, "Please leave!" I looked at his profile. "No," I answered. He looked me in the eye. "I want to be alone!" I returned his forceful gaze. "No," I answered sternly, and he lowered his hand, turned back to the water and whispered, "I want to be alone." I turned to the water, shook my head slowly, and said, "No."

We watched the water for a long while. Then, as he observed the water, I observed his eyes. When I noticed them filling with tears, I asked gently, "Are you okay, brother?" He swallowed a breath and nodded without looking at me and said, "I'm okay." I put my hand on his shoulder, he turned his eyes to it, and I continued, "You're not understanding me..." His eyes rose to meet my eyes. I asked slowly, "Are you okay, brother?" He grinned falsely and said, "I'm okay, brother." Then he let out a little laugh as if I were asking a ridiculous question. At that moment I shook my head and gripped his shoulder tightly and said in a most serious voice, "That's not what I'm asking, Amar. Amar, I'm asking you, are you okay?"

His eyes filled and a tear slipped down his cheek. He grew stern and angry. "Go away!" he demanded. I shook my head, for that was something I was no longer willing to do. "No," I said sternly and looked him straight in the eye to let him know that I would not abandon him. I would not let him be alone. I whispered, "Are you okay...brother?" He bared his teeth at me and said, "Leave!" I gripped him tighter and responded, "No!" I saw in his eyes despair as I had never seen or experienced before, despair so thick you could touch it, despair so heavy you could not even begin to imagine what had put it there. His eyes filled and he turned away. A memory was torturing his conscience. Then he turned back to me, grabbed my hand, and thrust it away. He said hoarsely, "When someone wants to be left alone, you leave! You leave them alone! You do not stay and ask...and ask....if..."

He stopped suddenly. His voice quivered and he was on the brink of tears. His lips tightened over his mouth and his brow lowered over his eyes. His eyes wrinkled and his lips began to tremble. He dropped his gaze to the floor and began to sob uncontrollably. Without hesitation, I took him in my arms and tried to soothe his pain. He shook and cried and kept on repeating, "I lost my soul." And every time he said the words I hushed him like a mother would hush her child. Then I told him that I didn't care what he had done, nor did I need to know. I told him that whatever it was that weighed so heavily on his heart, I took half away from him; I told him that from now on I bore half his pain, half his regret, half his burden, and that he no longer had to be alone.

We spent the whole night staring at the water in silence. When a new sun rose, Sunny approached us. At first he regarded us strangely, but then he joined our silence and watched the water. Ali and Sanjay approached us from the stern and followed suit. When men began to ascend the companionway and people the deck, Amar turned to Sunny,

75

and the two stared at each other for a short, thoughtful moment. Amar stared into Sunny's eyes and his eyes apologized. Sunny's eyes accepted humbly and, in turn, gleamed an apology. Amar's lips began to rise in a smile; then, all of a sudden, he startled us with a great laugh, grabbed Sunny, pulled him toward him and embraced him like a long lost brother. Ali raised his eyebrows in surprise and looked at Sanjay, who bore similar marks of surprise. Sunny gazed at me from Amar's chest with expressions of alarm, and then we all began to laugh. That laughter, after days of desolation and despair, was like the first sip of water after days of thirst under a relentless sun. We laughed and laughed and with the laughter we released weeks and weeks of accumulated pain, anger, and humiliation.

When our laughter subsided, Amar spotted some cooks preparing food outside. His eyes stared at the fire and seemed to know what to do. Slowly, he moved from us and made way for the cooking fire. Once there he pulled out his certificate and, crease by crease, unfolded it. He gave it one last look. We approached him from behind and formed a crescent around him. He looked to me, and I nodded my understanding. Finally, he thrust the certificate into the fire and watched the hungry flames devour it. As he watched the relentless flames leap and strike and throw the paper in all directions, the cooks stared at us with looks of sympathy and understanding. They watched the fire with us. They waited until the certificate was nothing more than ashes and smoke before they continued stirring and seasoning.

One of the cooks looked up to us, examined Amar's eyes for a moment, then said a most surprising thing. He said that soldiers had been burning up certificates and throwing medals in the water for the last two weeks and that every time they did so there was something that changed in their eyes, something he could see almost immediately. He wouldn't tell us what that change was, and said that he wasn't quite sure anyway, but that he definitely saw the change in Amar. I agreed with him. Amar seemed more alive--as if reborn--and all day he paced the deck at a militant stride, assessing our situation and searching his mind for solutions.

Amar spent the entire day cleaning the ship, and Sunny and I were the first to join his cleaning crusade. Sanjay, not wanting to be left out, eventually grabbed a rag and joined us. Soon, Ali gave up his bird hunt and joined us. As the day wore on, something strange happened. A remarkable thing happened. One by one, passengers joined our mission until the only ones who sat idle and did nothing were the sick and the weak. By evening, more than half of us were too busy scrubbing and re-scrubbing the deck to feel despair and by the time a crescent moon rose, the filth had been cleared and there lay on deck two distinct piles of garbage.

Proud of our work, we lay side by side enveloped by night listening to the strange insects. Amar said, "We must show these men we are not defeated. Tomorrow, when they walk aboard and see how we've changed the face of the ship, they will know, they will know we are not defeated." Sunny added with a laugh, "And that we'd make excellent maids." We all laughed at his comment. "Perhaps," said Amar, "But when they walk aboard…they will know…they will know that the battle is far from over."

Sunny looked over to me, then Amar, then me again, and his eyes went wide with disbelief as he tried his very best to determine where this new man had come from. I raised my eyebrows and feigned ignorance. But, in truth, I knew. I knew that we change everyday. Everyday we wake up as someone new, new because of the changes the day had made in us. Sometimes in little and hardly noticeable ways, sometimes in enormous and undeniable ways. But one cannot go through a day without changing a measure or two. My father used to go as far as to say that when we shut our eyes to sleep, the old us died and, as we slept, every sight, sound, smell, story, song, hymn, meal, conversation; everything that happened to us in the day, mixed and mingled with our soul and changed us so that, knowingly or unknowingly, we were different. He said that, depending on how we perceived those experiences, we'd either be stronger or weaker for them.

When my father shared this idea with me, I began to change, so that the next day I looked at everything with new eyes, forever searching for the way I would allow my experiences and encounters to change me.

And it wasn't long before I realized that your Grandfather was right: we die every day, and all experiences change you whether in slight or radical ways. The men who first arrived here no longer exist. They are dead. New men have now taken their place. Some have turned angry and bitter. They have changed for the worse. Others are stronger; they see this as a test, and every night they close their eyes on the dark day and thank Waheguru for the chance to shine through. And every night these men, these men who choose to change for the better, grow stronger and brighter and inspire all those around them. And because of these men, these men who refuse to change for the worse, who refuse to let the anarchists weaken their souls with their hate and anger, who refuse to lose the light, Nanak Jahaz is stronger, brighter, undefeated. For it is just as easy to spread the light as it is to smother it, and this is a ship of men who choose to spread it. That is why we will survive. That is why we will triumph.

June 30

We continued to clean all day, and by evening the lower deck and latrines were spotless. Observing the change in the men, Gurdit approached Amar and thanked him for his silent leadership. Amar smiled and then slowly turned his gaze to Ali, who was providing us with a kind of entertainment. Gurdit turned to Ali and watched him peculiarly. Ali crept toward a seagull like a lion on the prowl. Gurdit seemed puzzled. He turned to me, then to Amar, and then back to Ali. Then he turned to us and asked, "What is he doing?" Amar shrugged. Sanjay chuckled. Gurdit said, "Somebody tell him we still have food." Ali leapt at the seagull, but it escaped before he landed. Gurdit examined Ali for a moment, then concluded we had been on water for too long and maybe Ali should find some shade.

At night, exhausted by a hard and seemingly endless day of work, we fell asleep under a moonless sky, a sky so thick with haze that only one star shone through. The water was misty and choppy and the trees sighed and shook in the wind. The insects ceased their chirping and the night was oppressive and unforgiving. I stared at the star and it was as if it had been placed there just for me. To remind me that night couldn't last forever.

July 1

While we spent the morning cleaning the lower deck, Ali tried to catch a seagull using a fishing line he had found lying around the ship. He made a hook out of a nail, attached the line to it, then threw his invention at the birds in a feeble attempt to hook one. Fearful for our lives and the safety of the other passengers, Sanjay begged him to cease his attacks on the birds. Ali insisted he could catch one, but Sanjay assured him he no longer had anything to prove and could hurt someone with his hook. Ali explained that our food was diminishing and that he was more than sure Hopkinson and Moustache would try to starve us again. He said he refused to die of hunger, or to eat splinters of wood from the scow like he had heard others had done just a week ago. Fortunately, chasing birds and throwing the hook around the ship exhausted him, for by mid-afternoon he was sound asleep under the overhang in the coolness of shade. And no matter how hard Sanjay endeavoured to wake him, he would not wake.

July 2

This morning was unlike any other morning. Sunny and I opened our eyes to find Amar practicing Gartka, black against the rising sun. Sunny prodded me to make sure I was awake and witnessing what was nothing less than pure grace in the simple martial movements of an art very few of us knew or remembered. He moved in slow, concentrated semi-circles. With perfect balance, his every movement was graceful and circular so that he could deflect an opponent coming from any angle or direction. His feet moved forward and backward, his pace accelerated and deceler-ated, at last his feet made little quick stars and large evasive circles. In his hands he held an imaginary kirpan with which he sliced the air in complete and effortless movements. He turned at once slowly and sharply and his wrists moved in arcs while he turned and created openings between him and his imaginary opponent. At intervals he would stop abruptly and face the dawn and lose himself in meditation. Slowly, he would pick up his movements again, focusing his attention into his every movement. As I watched and admired him, Sunny signalled for me to look up at the housing. When I did I saw Gurdit and his boy, side by side, marvelling at Amar. At that moment I wished I had learned Gartka before my father died; then, at least, I would be able to teach you. Maybe I will ask Amar to teach you when you and your mother join me in Canada.

July 3

I wish you could see for yourself the change in the ship, in the men, and in Amar. I wish you could see the strength of will each man here possesses and carries with him like a golden torch. The ship is cleaner than it has ever been, and I still can't believe my eyes!

Today Hopkinson came aboard and I dare say his expression was one of shock and fear. He spent a few minutes examining Nanak Jahaz in silence, wondering, I suppose, if he had boarded the proper ship. He fixed his eyes on his men, and they returned his confounded look. Then his eyes swivelled from passenger to passenger, and every smile his eyes met caused a slight change within him. He saw things in us he had never seen before; he seemed worried and, at the same time, irritated. This incredible change in Nanak Jahaz caused a great stirring within him and he slowly began, unconsciously, to look at us differently. At last, whether he knew it or not, he looked and spoke and interacted with the passengers in an entirely different manner: there was newfound respect in his tone and a deep panic in his eyes; the panic of a man who takes a wrong turn in the jungle and finds himself surrounded by lions. And I think today he quite possibly realized that no matter how much the newspapers vilify us, and no matter how many laws they are willing to break to keep us prisoners in this cold, unfriendly sea, they would never succeed at imprisoning our souls. All this he saw and read in the new face of Nanak Jahaz. And the only time his malicious grin came out was when Gurdit told him we had run out of rations and that some of us, sick and undernourished, would not last another week without food.

Now I sit and stare at the pages of this yellowing journal and I think of you. My son, I hope you are working as hard as your mother and helping her in every chore; though I hope you are giving yourself plenty of time for play, so that you may remain healthy and strong-minded and ready for whatever calling Waheguru may have in store for you. And, no matter what the calling, may you always remain large-hearted, upright, and honest; and may you forever be concerned about others.

July 4

We are still anxiously awaiting the court's decision. I wonder if they're delaying on purpose. They know we have run out of food and that a few more days of hunger will, I'm afraid, devastate us. It's simply too much abuse for the body to bear and many are already bedridden. There is no greater obstacle than hunger and the anarchists know this. They know this all too well. Starving us has been their most effective weapon against us.

All day Amar and Ali were determined to catch us some food. Instead of chasing birds around the ship, they built a bird-trap with an old broken up, wooden box and a long piece of fishing line. They placed the box on deck and lifted it just high enough so a bird could fit underneath, and held the box up with a stick. With the fishing line tied to the stick, they waited a good distance away, hidden behind a lifeboat, hoping and waiting for a curious seagull to pass under and inspect the piece of glittering metal they had left under the trap. After a day of close calls, a seagull actually ventured under the box. But Amar and Ali were too busy talking and only noticed the bird when Sanjay screamed frantically for them to pull the line. By the time they reacted and the box fell it was too late, and the seagull was high in the sky drifting away on a gentle breeze.

July 5

Today we heard terrible news from Gurdit. A few local Indians were beaten and humiliated by an angry mob and the authorities will do nothing for them. What's more is the newspapers didn't even report the incident. I suppose such an incident is not worthy news; I suppose such an incident might possibly evoke pity for Indians from the good people of Vancouver; and I suppose those in charge of general opinion do not wish for anyone to sympathise with us. Though I imagine, had the situation been reversed, the story would have made front page news for weeks on end. What incredible power! What incredible influence! To control the opinions, conversations, and table-talk of an entire community! The shore committee says things are becoming worse and worse in Vancouver. Everyone is petrified of Indians, and Indians can no longer walk the streets alone. They must always be in groups for fear of being beaten or lynched. I despise the newspapers and feel a profound pity for the men who write for them, men who sacrifice truth and spread the contagion purely for the possibility of being published. If there is one thing I understand better these days, it's the old Arab proverb that states: "When the King puts the poet on his payroll, he cuts the tongue of the poet." Nothing could be closer to the truth.

In the evening, Amar told us that had the Romans had newspapers they would probably still exist and most likely still be in power. He told us that their way of controlling the masses was through circus games, which they used like the British now use the newspapers: to promote political campaigns, leaders, and Emperors; to spread selectively chosen news that glorified themselves and beastified others; and to spread a collective fear of Christians and barbarians to get the people's minds off their hunger. Then he went on to tell us that there was once an Emperor who actually burned down his city to make room for a garden and a palace that his senators rejected due to a lack of space. He levelled the city and murdered his own people to create the space and, to quash the people's anger for the massacre of so many fellow Romans, he found a scapegoat in the Christians. He spread his false opinions and accusations at the circus games where Christians were consequently thrown to the beasts by the thousands. Years later, it was discovered that it was, in fact, the Emperor who had burned down the city, that it was he who had burnt and slaughtered his own people, who had used the games to spread lies and redirect the people's anger. The Emperor was condemned by the senate to be flogged to death, but in the end, terrified of facing his own people, he took his own life. Ultimately, the words and speeches spoken at the games were no longer trusted. And this, Amar believes, marked the beginning of the end of the Roman Empire: when Romans began to realize that the only truths they would ever be exposed to were those that justified the actions of the Emperor.

We were all taken aback that an Emperor would murder his own people for a mere garden. Amar explained that it was quite common and that history would always repeat itself. He said that the only thing that would change would be the stage and the actors. At this Sunny nodded, and then he interjected his own little story. "My father," he said, "once told the village a very similar story." He paused, scanned our faces, and then continued without interruption:

"There was once an Emperor who wanted to increase his empire and treasury by invading foreign lands rich with diamonds. But none of his subjects would agree to such acts, as they were relatively peaceful and thought their taxes would be better spent on reducing hunger and poverty within their own empire. So the Emperor consulted his advisors. It was agreed that the only way to fulfill his wishes without damaging his good name was to create an atmosphere of fear and terror. So the Emperor approached the leader of the barbarians and paid him a substantial amount in gold and weapons to attack his cities. When the carnage was over and terror was everywhere, the Emperor had the barbarian leader exterminated. In less than a week he had his subjects exactly where he wanted them: screaming for vengeance, voting for war. Soon he had the army he had always dreamed of along with the only reason he would ever need to use that army to steal the wealth of other lands."

July 6

We must leave! Moustache and Hopkinson refused to allow our lawyer to see or speak with Gurdit in private, so our lawyer screamed the verdict from the immigration launch so that all the immigration officials could hear his awful words and the humiliation was intensified. Since it was difficult to hear him, he had to repeat the verdict several times. Now, despair and hunger have taken prisoner of everyone's face, and slowly the light is being smothered. However, Amar refuses to let anyone sulk or despair. He says we must stay strong for the friends and families we have left behind, and, if not for them, then at least for Nanak Jahaz, for Gurdit and the passengers, for the family we've become. Waheguru stay with us; keep us strong.

July 7

Everyone is ill, weak, and demoralized; and our only sickness is hunger. Hopkinson came aboard with a woman who was writing down all of his arrogant words. I wonder if she wrote down that no one could understand a single word of his poor, poor mingled Hindi-Punjabi, nor could we understand the words of the other man he had brought with him. I wonder if these immigration officers understand that there is a difference between Hindi and Punjabi, that they are not the same languages. I suppose they don't. All Indians are Hindus to them, and all Hindus speak Hindi. Usually we would derive intense amusement from his butchering of Punjabi and Hindi, and how he constantly mixes the two languages up, but now no one laughs. Some of us are just too hungry to laugh, while most of us realize the dire consequences of his butchering. I observed the woman and wondered if she wrote down that he looked upon our suffering with a smile. He seemed more than pleased with the new face of the ship.

Gurdit requested food and water, and it almost seemed as though he was restraining himself from pouncing on Hopkinson, for Hopkinson continued to smile at our defeat as though rubbing salt into our wounds for the pleasure of hearing us scream. As he walked across the sun-drenched deck, a passenger rushed up to him and said in Punjabi that his friends needed food and water, that they would surely die without rations, and that if he could simply put himself in our situation he would surely make provisioning Nanak Jahaz his first priority. But as the man spoke, Hopkinson became terribly irritated and frustrated with his inability to understand. As a result, he pushed the begging man out of his way before anyone could realize his inabilities. Hopkinson acting as translator for them is like Gurdit acting as translator for the captain. He may have learned a few Japanese words here and there but Gurdit in no way understands the language. And now, I wonder how much this man has fabricated in his ignorance and how much influence he has had on our lives. I feel a great anger surging within me. I will stop writing.

July 8

I'm sorry if this is illegible, my son, but there is no life in me, in my body, in my arm, in my hand. Hunger has now taken its toll, and I'm afraid it's more than I can bear. Amar and a few other ex-soldiers are the only ones who seem to have the energy to do anything. I suppose they are used to these kinds of conditions. This morning Amar taught Gartka to Gurdit's boy; they were beautiful to watch. At least Gurdit and his boy still have food, little as it may be.

Amar and Ali sat by their trap all afternoon praying for a bird, but no bird came. In fact, birds stayed as far away from the ship as possible, sensing, I suppose, our hunger. When night descended and the stars came out, Amar tried to persuade Sunny to tell a story, any story, but Sunny, try as he did, could hardly speak for a total lack of moisture in his mouth. When he tried to speak, white paste formed at the corners of his mouth as he forced his lips to move. But there was no focus or order in his words and soon, when the corners of his mouth cracked and began to bleed, Amar realized his mistake, put his hand on Sunny's shoulder, and, with his eyes, pleaded for him to stop. Sunny lowered his head and fell painfully silent.

July 9

Moustache came aboard today and, seeing our situation and sensing death on the horizon, did what Hopkinson refused to do. He supplied us with water and a day's worth of food, which we are going to try to conserve for the next three days, or week if we can. He then told Gurdit he would only further provision the ship when we were ready to leave. Gurdit told him it was out of his hands now and we would only leave when all the passengers agreed to leave. So, I suppose, they will continue to try and starve us home, but, really, this would make more sense if there were food to go home to!

July 10

Many men are sick from the food and Gurdit suspects foul play, but Amar says these last few months have destroyed our stomachs and any food will prove difficult, if not impossible, to digest. Apparently, any food, fresh or rotten, will render many of us sick. But even he hasn't completely ruled out the possibility of foul play. We, however, are stronger from the food, so we tend to the sick and clean whatever needs to be cleaned. In the evening, Ali claimed he nearly caught a seagull, and Sanjay said "nearly" didn't quite "fry the samosa" or get his family off the eternal laundry hook! We laughed at that. It was the first time in a while that we had laughed, and it felt good, really good. But just as soon as we ceased our laughter, Sunny became solemnly serious as he reported yet another rumour about Hopkinson, which he had heard from another passenger.

I have never heard so many awful stories about a single man in my life. Apparently, there is a man in San Francisco who is determined to assassinate Hopkinson for having taken a bribe and not fulfilled his part of the promise, which was to pass his wife's interview and let her into the country. But before Sunny could finish recounting the rumour, Sanjay interrupted him and said he had heard an entirely different version of the same story. He said the man's motivation had nothing to do with a bribe but with an attempt to rape his wife and that, while giving her the interview, he closed the office door, held the interview assessment papers up to her, and said if she wanted to see her husband again she knew what she had to do. She stood up and chose to return home, unable to explain to the other English authorities what had taken place. At that moment we all closed our eyes, imagined our wives in a similar situation, and the rage blood pounded. We knew this was a common blackmail among men with power, especially among those men who had some sort of control over a woman's fate. We had all heard too many similar stories about British authorities and Indian women to merely dismiss this one as a rumour. And when I thought of Hopkinson's malicious smile and how he looked at us and seemed to despise every ounce of us, I knew there was more truth to the rumour than exaggeration.

After a long, breathless silence, Sunny said, "May that paleface get his medicine!" He was very emotional, as if his own wife or sister or mother had experienced a similar situation. "Don't say that," I said, turning to him, trying to prevent anger and hate from blinding his reason. But it was too late. "Why not!" he demanded, "It is because of him I am not landed! Corrupt! Corrupt! Corrupt! If I had the money I'd be landed, too! He shouldn't have power!" He paused, searched for a thought, then, his eyes wide and white, continued, "You once said some men shouldn't have power! And that they force and use power for evil things and do so against power's will...and you said that one day that very abuse would come back to them and tear them apart...I hope it tears him apart...limb by limb! I hope it tears him apart!" I shook my head and saw the hell in his eyes. He continued like a man possessed. "You will write about this?" he asked with burning eyes. I nodded my answer. "Good!" he said, "Then tell your son that when he gets his medicine, and the newspapers make him a martyr...you make sure your son knows what he really was...an animal! Nothing more than an animal!"

He paused and reflected on his words. Then he changed his mind. "No!" he said, "Not an animal! Worse! Animals don't do these things to their own." He shook his head and repeated in a whisper, "Animals don't do these things to their own." He fell silent; then, as an afterthought, he looked up at me and said, "You write about him and how he starved us and laughed at our suffering, so at least, when the newspapers misrepresent everything, your son will know the truth." I nodded. He was in hell and there was no sense reasoning with him. I told myself I would talk to him tomorrow and maybe save him from committing the crime I could see burning in the depths of his mind.

July 11

There is another awful rumour going around. Passengers are whispering that the immigration officers are planning to board the ship with the navy and slaughter us for refusing to retreat. The rumour has taken root in all of our hearts and fear--I wish it weren't true--has overwhelmed many. How sad it will be to see British soldiers fight British soldiers. But there will be no fight, for what can we fight with? And with what strength? There is only a little bit of food left and very little water.

In the evening the men continued to whisper stories about Hopkinson. Most of them are just plain absurd but, then again, maybe they are not as absurd as what has been written about us in the newspapers. I suppose the stories do not bother me so much, but what does bother me is their constant use of "paleface". Sunny uses this word all the time, and when he does, it's as though I can no longer think about a man with hopes and dreams and friends and family like me, I can only think of a beast that commands no respect or compassion or humanity. And it is much easier to accept that it is heartless palefaces who are putting us through this rather than men. Surely men couldn't do this to other men. But a paleface, well, a paleface is capable of all kinds of nameless horrors.

July 12

Fear is crippling. The passengers are almost destroyed by the idea of being slaughtered by their own comrades in a place so foreign and cold to their hearts. The ship is filthy again now and many of us just want to go home. Gurdit should talk to us, reinforce our spirits, but he himself is at a loss for what to do. He merely sits in his cabin staring out the window wondering, possibly, why this had to happen to us.

I heard a man cry like a baby last night. He cried throughout the night and stopped only when there were no more tears left in him. His sobbing rose above the pain-filled cries of the sick and the hungry and echoed throughout the entire ship. I wonder if they could even hear his cries on the immigration launch and, if they did, I wonder if it affected them in any way. Probably not; our tears aren't real to them.

I wish they would allow provisions through. We can hardly move and I'm having troubles writing again. Sunny is incoherent and he hasn't spoken to himself for weeks now. There was a man who nearly died of dehydration and when Sunny took his last sip of water and made the man drink it, he looked to me and said, "If he dies, the paleface is to blame!" Later that night I asked him why he always had to call them that. He looked at me as if I were crazy for having asked such a question. But then, when he tried to answer, he found he was unable to. He said, "I call them that because…I'm not sure…just feels good, that's all." Then Amar, who we thought was asleep but who was in fact listening to our conversation, interjected what I already knew. "It's a security word," he said plainly. "That's why you use it." He turned to Sunny and me and then continued, "You use that word to drain the man of Waheguru. It's something you do to make killing or hurting or abusing easier. It's a security word. That's all it is. It makes the cruelty okay even though your heart screams it's not. Though, you use a security word long enough, you find your heart only whispers its revolt…eventually it stops interfering altogether." He seemed to be speaking from experience.

I thought about his words all night and I soon realized what I had always known: our lives are in the image of Waheguru and we should always love and see Waheguru everywhere and in everything. And anything we choose to deprive of Waheguru immediately dies to us. For races are enslaved by others by first depriving men of Waheguru. That is what they have done to us, they have deprived us of Waheguru; and to accept what they have done to us, we have done it to them.

July 14

Sick, starving, and exhausted, no one can move. Heads are down and
thoughts are inward. When passengers do talk, they talk of home and
whisper they do not wish to die in this cold, windy, miserable place.
Some men search the water with hungry eyes, hoping for dead fish; and
I've heard some men have again resorted to eating splinters from the
scow. Ali sits hidden behind a lifeboat, anxiously watching his trap and
the birds in the sky. Sanjay prays he catches one. I'm so weak I can barely do anything except watch the sky and think of you. I miss you so
much. I miss all our shared smiles and laughs and I pray this will all be
over soon and I will be holding you in my arms. Forgive me if I hold you
for what will surely feel like forever! For this is what this separation feels
like, forever. But you've been with me all along, and your mother has
always had the most wonderful ideas. For this journal has helped me in
ways I can hardly express. It keeps my mind clear and focused, and it
often helps me rid myself of negativity. It affords me the chance to think
about things, to re-tread past events in my mind, and there is something
about putting what I'm going through on paper that is calming, healing,
soothing to my soul. Soon I will close the journal, and then I will shut
my eyes, and we will be together again: playing in the field; watching
people at the bazaar; enjoying your mother's daal-rotis; watching the stars
on clear and most divine nights. I should stop thinking about these things
now. I miss you so very much, and I feel crazy enough to jump in the
water and swim home!

July 15

Amar is an incredible man. I can hardly keep up with him. No one can,
and I wonder where he gets all his strength from. This afternoon he came
up to me as I lay in the shade and gave me a little kick. He asked me if I
was sick. I told him I was just weak and conserving my energy. Then he
said that would have been a fine answer if others weren't in distress. But,
since dozens were practically on their deathbed, we needed to do whatever we could to help them. He then told me to conserve my energy below

90

deck with the sick, to which I responded that I was useless without food or water or supplies. To this he shook his head and said our mere presence was enough because all they needed was to see that someone cared and was there for them. Moments later, as we made our way below deck, he turned to me and said, "No one should be alone." I spent the whole day holding a stranger's hand. I tried to talk to the poor man, but he was too sick to respond in any way. He tried to thank me, but I soon stifled his pitiful attempt.

Later that day, as the sun began to make its descent and the light outside began to fade, a man stood black against the companionway where a mellow light poured in from behind him. He held a man limp in his arms and, before I could make out his silhouette, he called out for Amar. I immediately recognized the voice. It was Sanjay. He carried Ali in his arms and brought him to a bunk close to the other sick men. As Amar tried to help him, prodding for signs of life, Sanjay explained what had taken place. When he went to check on Ali and his trap, he was shocked to find a bird sitting in the shade of the box. He shouted for Ali to pull the fishing line, but there was no response. With his eyes, he followed the line from the box to the lifeboat. Again he shouted for Ali to pull the string. Again no response. He screamed as loud as his lungs would permit and, when the bird flew away, he began to curse and call Ali names, swearing he must want all of us to starve. But when he rounded the lifeboat to admonish his friend, he swallowed all his bitter words and rushed to his side, for Ali was sprawled over the deck, unconscious, with his tongue thick and swollen in his throat.

Sanjay spent the whole night by Ali's side. I came to sit beside him, and he said to me, "He needs water." I nodded. He swore a terrible curse, and then asked if I could stay with Ali for a moment. I nodded, and he rose and made for the upper deck. It wasn't long before I heard him shuffling about, begging passengers for water with no success. Then he went silent. After a long while he returned with a cup of seawater. He went to pour the cup's contents into Ali's mouth, but I leapt for his hand, grabbed his wrist tightly, looked him straight in the eye, and told him he could not give him the saltwater, that it would only worsen his condition or possibly kill him. He dropped the cup and said, "I need water!" I looked at him and said, "I am sorry!" His eyes widened frantically.

"Sorry," he yelled hoarsely, "doesn't help!" And he bolted back up the companionway where I could hear him cursing at the immigration launch, screaming for water at the top of his lungs. When he had exhausted himself, he returned below deck and sat beside me, staring at Ali's skeletal face. He said, "If anything happens to him..." But he couldn't finish his sentence. He just shook his head miserably. After a moment, he grabbed Ali's hand. "It's going to be okay...you hear me...can you hear me, brother? I'm not going to leave you. I'm not going to leave you." And he never did.

July 16

Moustache and Hopkinson boarded this morning and, as they stepped aboard Nanak Jahaz, Gurdit's boy darted down the companionway and whispered something in Sanjay's ear. In an instant Sanjay was up on deck, storming toward them with lethal intent. But, luckily for the immigration officers, Amar, recognizing the intent, grabbed him before he could do any damage. Sanjay struggled and squirmed and screamed for him to let go, and Sunny and I ran to Amar's aid to help restrain him. Realizing he couldn't break free from our hold, Sanjay screamed at the officers in a language they couldn't understand, "If my friend dies, I'll kill you! If he dies, you die! Do you hear! Do you understand! You heartless cowards!" They stared at us blankly. Hopkinson smiled at us, and Sanjay yelled for him to wipe his grin off his face. Eventually we dragged an exhausted Sanjay below deck, and did so before he could incite a riot. It was some time before he was calm again and, when he was, he asked Sunny, "Can you...can you maybe tell him a story. Anything, doesn't matter. Just so it makes him feel better. Maybe it will help him forget about this place." Sunny gazed thoughtfully at Ali: his face was listless and pale; his eyes were wide open but did not see; his mouth was slightly open but did not smile or frown. He just stared lifelessly into space, the emptiness of his stare pulling at our souls. Sunny grabbed Ali's arm and turned to Sanjay and said, "Sure I will, brother. Sure, I will..." And he sat beside Ali and told him a story.

That evening Gurdit made an announcement. Much to our disapproval, he had made a deal with Hopkinson. He would allow the doctor to leave on the condition they would give us some water in return. One passenger said harshly, "He will say things against us!" Gurdit answered, "We need water." The passenger continued, "He should stay!" Gurdit, with mixed anger and frustration rising in his throat, said, "We need water!" The passenger responded, "He should not go!" Gurdit walked up to the passenger, looked him straight in the eye, and, pronouncing each and every syllable, said, "We need water!" The man's head sank; all of our heads sank. He was right. We need water.

July 17

The traitor was escorted off Nanak Jahaz and many passengers waved their shoes and sandals at him. Once the doctor was secure on land, water was pumped on board. And that day each of us spent hours upon hours savouring just a few sips of water. Many of us now feel a degree better, but still there is a general lack of strength and vitality. Many lie around the ship defeated and demoralized, worrying about the battle to come.

While Amar stayed below taking care of the sick, and Sanjay sat by Ali's side praying for his quick recovery, Sunny and I spent the afternoon cleaning the deck and emptying the latrines with a few other passengers: those who refused to be defeated. Today Gurdit and his boy helped us scrub the deck. As we scrubbed, Gurdit, without raising his eyes at me, said, "Sometimes when I'm in a mess I start cleaning and, somehow, it is strange, but somehow the answer comes to me." He sighed a great sigh of disappointment, then continued in a discouraged voice. "But not this time. This time I don't know what to do…if they storm the ship…" I stopped scrubbing to look up at him. He stopped scrubbing. He stared at me with wet eyes, shook his head gravely, and said flatly, "We don't stand a chance."

Everything can change in a day. From sunrise to sunset this was the most sorrowful ship you could possibly imagine. All day Amar paced the ship looking at the defeated faces, examining each one carefully to see if there was hope left in any of them. Finding none, he wore his own sombre face of disappointment. Hunger and fear had finally taken its toll on the men; their spirits were low, and their leader, to whom they looked for strength, was beginning to show signs of defeat. Gurdit had isolated himself in his cabin, and he held his head in his hands all day, worrying, for he knew the slaughter was soon to come. His boy merely watched and comforted his father and said nothing; for there was nothing to say and there was no comfort in words of comfort. Amar paced the ship until the fearful whispers and whimpers of the men struck his soul like a bolt of lightening and sent him thundering across the ship with his hands extended to the heavens.

He pointed at the men and yelled over and over again, "What is this! What is this! Are we dead or are we alive!" No one responded, but the whimpering and the whispers ceased. Amar yelled, "Are we defeated? Is that it? Are we!" Still, no one answered. "Well," he exclaimed, "I'm not. I'm not dead! And as long as I'm not dead, I will fight!" Then he turned round and round looking at the men to see if anyone was prepared to join him. No one met his gaze and all lips were sealed. He asked, "Is there anyone on this ship who is alive?" His fiery eyes swept the men. He continued, "Is there anyone else who will fight?" At that moment a man stood, slammed his chest, and said, "I am alive!" And he walked toward Amar and stood beside him. Then another followed and shouted, "I, too, am alive!" And he took his place beside Amar. They waited for more men to join them, but no one else stood. Out of all of us only two men had risen while the rest of us just lay across the deck in resigned silence waiting for the darkness to descend. Amar turned to me, and I stood and took my place beside him. The other two men patted my shoulder and praised my courage.

Amar turned round and round and met everyone's gaze one at a time. Gurdit and his boy stepped out of their cabin and watched us from above. Amar demanded, "Should we just let them board and slaughter us like pigs? Is this what you're telling me?" A passenger yelled, "No, we should just go home…to our families!" Amar stared at the passenger for a moment and then played with the word, "Home…home…home? Yes, ahhh…you mean you still believe we have a place we can call our home?" Amar laughed a loud and false laugh which squeezed and twisted our hearts. We knew he was right. He stopped laughing and continued, "Has this taught you anything, brother? Has it! We have no home, brothers. Our families have no home. Indians have no home! And so long as we refuse to stand up for our rights, we will never have a home. No, brothers, we shrink from their threat now and they will forever threaten us…our wives…our children…our grandchildren! Shrink from their threat and they will forever threaten us and treat our people like dogs! In our home! Is that what you want?" The passenger lowered his eyes. Amar began to point at the passengers one at a time; each time he pointed at someone he asked them the same question and each one met him with the same resigned silence. No one seemed moved by his words. Their fear was too intense and it had made an impenetrable shield against their hearts. Amar said, "Since when do we shrink from the tyrant? Since when!" The words struck the shield and fell useless to the floor. A passenger shouted, "We haven't any weapons!" Another shouted, "I want to see my family!" Disappointed, Amar shook his head and asked, "Who will stand with me against the tyrant?"

There was a long silence. No one stood. No one said a word. No one showed any sign of courage or strength. Amar shook his head, and the whispers began. The men whispered their fears about how they hadn't any strength or weapons to fight with, and how the soldiers would surely come with rifles and bayonets. Amar's head began to sink, and my head soon followed suit when all of a sudden, from above, came a commanding voice that drifted to us in song and filled us all with alarm. Gurdit's boy had begun to sing a hymn and, as he sang, slowly made his way toward Amar. It wasn't long before the boy was in the middle of the deck and others had begun to sing with him. The hymn rose over the shields, seeped into their hearts, and before long was on all lips. Everyone was standing and singing with their eyes closed; and those who were too sick to stand or sing made silent movements with their lips. The hymn had a hypnotic effect; the sounds of the world around us receded, and anxious, panic-stricken hearts began to slow. Those beautiful words penetrated my heart and made a chill of courage climb my spine. Slowly, the hymn freed us from our prison of fear, and Nanak Jahaz began to fill with the strength and selfless courage of our ancestors. The rest of the night was spent preparing for battle.

July 19

It happened early this morning before sunrise. Singing hymns, sometimes loud, sometimes in a whisper, but all the time keeping our hearts and heads filled with the courageous words and deeds of our ancestors, we prepared piles of coal by the rail. And it was as we brought the coal closer to the rail when Amar suddenly threw his hand up in the air and hushed everyone quiet. At first no one heard anything. There was only the silence of night. Then we heard it. We immediately recognized the grunting sound. The grunting and groaning sound of an engine. Then there was hushed laughter, laughter coming from the source of the grunting, which steadily increased in intensity. We leaned over the rail and saw a tug filled with policemen and soldiers who were laughing and joking amongst themselves, laughing as if their mission were a sort of picnic or practice of little or no consequence. From their tug a searchlight illuminated the water. The bright circle lit up the water and then wandered from its black surface to the rusty side of our ship. The light then moved its way up to the rail where passengers leaned over and bravely watched them. With the light almost blinding us, we could hardly see them. We only saw dark shadows waving guns at us. And this sight, coupled with the blinding light and the maddening hunger, made me want to jump onto the tug and battle them all myself.

A passenger laughed at the tug and yelled, "This is their navy?" To which Amar, never taking his eyes off the tug, replied, "A hundred guns!" He then squinted and turned to Gurdit. Gurdit regarded him a moment and then raised his eyes to the heavens and prayed, "Waheguru...make us fast and accurate." Then Amar looked up to the same sky, adding, "And unstoppable." I observed the hundred or so passengers around me and saw deep in their eyes an infinite strength. I immediately knew this would be no pig slaughter. They would have a fight. And they would soon cease their laughter.

There was a long silence as we stared down at them and they stared back up at us. Then, breaking the silence, a passenger yelled out to Hopkinson and told him that this was all his fault, that all of this could have been avoided with a little justice, a little truth, a little diplomacy. Hopkinson laughed at the man and said something that we only understood in bits and parts. Another man attempted Punjabi with the same result. Then a passenger yelled, "This is the incompetence we've been dealing with! These are the decision makers! It's no wonder it has come down to this!" Another passenger yelled at Hopkinson and challenged him to recite the Punjabi alphabet. Hopkinson responded with a blank, helpless look. Another passenger added, "Yes, if you say it, we'll start the engine and go back home!" Gurdit turned to the passenger, upset that he had made such a promise.

There was a restless silence. A chill of anxiety ran down my spine. Hopkinson looked up at us as if he were actually going to recite the Punjabi alphabet. We waited restlessly for Hopkinson's reply. After a moment, Hopkinson turned his back on us, edged up to Moustache, and whispered something in his ear. Moustache turned and barked out rapid-fire commands. At once his men prepared their weapons, and we braced ourselves for battle. Now we knew one of two things: either Hopkinson wanted us all dead, or he really didn't understand Punjabi. Either way, it didn't matter. We were ready to return their aggression.

Gurdit lifted his hand and we all held a piece of coal firmly in our hands. He said, "Make ready!" And we raised the coal over our heads. Moustache yelled a command and suddenly a fire hose was on us, trying to push us away from the rail; but no sooner had their aggression begun than Gurdit gave the command. A black storm ravaged them. We pelted coal down at them and didn't stop for fifteen minutes. We feared the guns and we feared the bullets and we felt that one moment of respite would afford them the chance to aim and fire and kill. We allowed them no such opportunity. Our ammunition was abundant, and abundant because of their own underhanded ways! Had they respected the laws and allowed Gurdit to sell his coal, we would have had nothing to fight with. But everything happens for a reason and today we understand the reason;

these anarchists are defeated by their own vice.

The dark avalanche, camouflaged by night, smashed the lights and the windows and battered the tug mercilessly. Twice they almost tipped over as they, in their panic and confusion, all ran to the same side. They were frantically running all over the tug like headless chickens, screaming for their lives. Eventually they all hid in the captain's cabin, and the man who held the hose on us dropped it as he, too, ran for cover. The tug filled with coal and the men cried like lost children. They begged and pleaded with their superiors to get them out of harm's way, but the tug was attached to our ship by grapple and line and none of those soldiers were brave enough to enter our fire to cut themselves free. Ultimately, one man, possibly the only brave one of the lot, ran to the bow and cut the line that attached us to them. Then he ran back to the cabin and they hastened into a full retreat. As they crawled back to shore, defeated, we roared our victory. Sunny threw both hands in the air and screamed, "Behold!" He paused and turned to us with smiling eyes. He yelled gloriously, "The great lions!" At his words we cheered uncontrollably, and Gurdit threw his boy on his shoulders, and his boy led us in song.

July 20

Now only six men are bedridden. Sanjay spends all his time with Ali who shows no apparent sign of improvement. All day Sunny told and retold the story of the battle to the sick men. In the dim lantern light below deck, he was alive with his story; his eyebrows rose and fell with the rhythm of the story, and he paused with intense facial expressions just when he knew the men wanted more. And only when he sensed they could take no more did he continue. Quite often he purposely left things out, as he always did with his stories, for he knew some things were better left unexplained and, for the most part, he couldn't do better than his audience's imagination. When he told the story he became the story and, with the exception of the things he purposely left out, he dressed the story up so much that you actually felt you were there. Every detail he used succeeded at hooking our imaginations to his so that those who had not been there might speak about the battle as if they had. And more than once he drew glorious smiles out of the sick men and thus received the only payment he sought for his efforts.

July 21

There is a battleship in the harbour and scattered all over the water are little skiffs and fishing boats filled with people looking for a little excitement to fill their monotonous lives. I have never seen so many people crowded along the shore, nearly spilling into the water, pointing and staring out at our ship and the battleship, as if we were a kind of sea monster and the battleship were a knight in shining armour here to defeat us once and for all. Gurdit gathered us and told us that after their humiliating defeat he had expected this, and that now they were ready to fill this sea with our blood.

A delegation of local Indians came out to reason with us. They brought us a little food and water, which was immediately taken to the sick. They said the food and water was sent by the government, and we immediately knew Moustache and Hopkinson were no longer in charge. The men boarded Nanak Jahaz, and Gurdit led them to his cabin where they deliberated for over an hour. When they came to a solution, a peaceful solution, the men re-boarded their launch and returned to shore. Gurdit announced that they had worked something out. Nanak Jahaz would be well-provisioned for a journey back to India where we would seek redress for time and money lost during the last three months, including money sacrificed by the shore committee on provisions and a lawyer, which would have been unnecessary had the immigration authorities been loyal and honest and followed the laws. The Indian community would eventually get all their money back, they promised. One passenger yelled we would never see justice and we would never get our money back from the government. He said all the money the shore committee had collected and sacrificed was lost, and that the tyrant would promise to pay in the future, but would conveniently forget, and when the Indian committee sought what was rightfully theirs, the tyrant would find every excuse possible to avoid compensation. They would most likely point to all the lies

Hopkinson and the doctor had fabricated as reasons for non-payment, and purposely forget the truth of Munshi Singh, the father and farmer who represented the three hundred passengers and who had suffered and lost everything as consequence of those fabrications.

Gurdit fell silent at his words; he knew the man was right. There would be no compensation and all this suffering had been in vain. He didn't seem to know what to do or say. He turned from us and went back to his cabin. He thought about the man's observations and returned at sunset with something of a speech prepared. We gathered around him and, as the wind howled around us, he spoke with emotion and colour: "My brothers," he said with a great smile, "you have no idea how proud I am to be here with you. I am the luckiest man alive! You, in the last three months have taught me more about myself, about my own people, than I could ever have hoped to learn in a lifetime of security and comfort, isolated and separated from my neighbours." He paused, and his eyes swept over all of us before he continued. "For it is only in the toughest and the most trying of circumstances that the true colours of the soul come out...and brothers...oh, brothers!...you have shown me gold!"

The air resounded with the word. He stopped, and a glorious smile was on him again, glowing, blessing, inspiring. He extended his hands to all of us and said, "I tell you this!" His face went serious. "Pick any time in history, pick any place in the world, and I would not choose any other time, I would not choose any other place...and I would most certainly not choose any other group of men to suffer with! Gold! All of you, gold!" Slowly, he moved about the passengers and, as he gazed at each man, he pointed, stating, "Gold!" And our hearts filled with the word. Finally, he stood still and continued with warmth and richness and passion, and he owned everyone's undivided attention. "They say sometimes bad things happen for good reasons. I've been searching for those reasons. I've been searching and searching and trying to understand. I've been trying so hard for the last few weeks to understand why we were brought here, why we had to see what we had to see, learn what we had to learn, and, until today, brothers, I had no answer. But today, brothers, in a newspaper a man brought for me, I read the reason."

He paused, made sure he had everyone's attention, and then he continued with a face the very picture of seriousness. "In Europe there is a great war on the horizon. The war of wars! The mother of wars…that is what it is being called. Can you see, brothers, what I see?" An unnamed feeling stole over us. The men began to shift uneasily. Some began to murmur amongst themselves. Gurdit closed his eyes and, making elaborate gestures with his hands, bellowed, "I see mountains of our people, slaughtered! Unrecognizable! One piled on top of the other! Men who sacrificed their lives, women who sacrificed their husbands, boys and girls who sacrificed their fathers for land that will never be theirs." A great commotion rippled through the passengers. Gurdit opened his eyes with a start, and his eyes were on all of us. "I can see no greater lesson than the lesson we learned here: the lesson of who we really are within this Empire. And what we are not is subjects! And so long as our skin is brown we will never be treated as subjects and will forever be treated as lepers! And if I am a leper and not a subject of this Empire, I will not die for it! My fellow countrymen will not die for it! My son will not die for it!" His words echoed throughout the ship and charged everyone with purpose and determination.

"Neither mine!" protested a passenger.

"Nor mine!" yelled another.

"I will die before my son kills another man for this King!" yelled yet another.

Soon every man was yelling the same thing.

Gurdit's eyes ran along their rigid faces. He lifted his hand and gestured for silence. In a moment all was silent. He said sharply, "This is why I have gathered you here. You have experienced the power and strength of men who bond and stick together. You have learned the lesson. And now it seems futile to die here fighting foolishly against a battleship when there is such an important lesson to be shared and spread back home. We are the bearers of truth, and with this truth we shall free our country." Suddenly we realized why Gurdit had so easily capitulated to the anarchists. He wasn't scared of their floating war machine. From deep within him a new calling had emerged: a calling that necessitated our safe return. He continued passionately, "How, I wonder, can we convince three hundred million people to stop trying to be like those who enslave them, to stop fighting amongst themselves, and to take back what is rightfully theirs?" His eyes moved from one passenger to the other.

"How, I wonder, do we teach three hundred million Indians the way to overcome the tyrant?" He smiled, lifted his hand, and exclaimed, "By teaching him how three hundred did it! By first freeing them from themselves! By convincing them to stop chasing the illusions of the Maya!" He stopped, shook his head, and then continued, "Indians collaborate in their own enslavement...for false respectability and status they provide the King with the police and soldiers he needs to enforce his will; his will to reduce us to such a degraded state of dependency that we cannot even feed our own children...make our own clothes...produce our own salt!"

He paused to watch the faces, the reactions, and the eyes. Every man was ablaze. He continued, "They systematically plunder India's wealth. They deprive us of all our natural resources so that our factories and farms wither away while their factories and farms flourish. Then their newspapers call us uneducated and uncivilized for not being able to take care of our own. They call us uncivilized for the very problems they create! And then they act as if they are doing us some great favour by teaching us how to do things the civilized way; by sending us back food that they themselves have stolen from our plates." He cackled. "The civilized way, apparently, is to steal the chicken and return the bones." His laugh grew louder and he began to shake his head. "Then Indians, who are taught from childhood to believe in and trust the tyrant's tool, read these newspapers and believe so much in them that they are convinced both of their master's superiority and of their own inferiority. They become riddled with insecurities and lose their inner strength, becoming easier to control than dogs. And so they are treated like dogs!"

There was a long reflective silence. After a moment Gurdit held up a newspaper and said, "They read these newspapers and are convinced that they need things they do not need, that they should be more like Englishmen. And trying so hard to be like an English gentleman, the Indian spends his whole life too distracted to see the tyrant's evils and misdeeds, as he forever chases the tyrant's definition of civilized living. I propose we return..."

A passenger broke in, "And make them pay in blood!"

"Make them pay!"

"No," said Gurdit, shaking his head. "That is not the way. I am after total liberation, not a small, meaningless victory. Total liberation! Violence will fail as violence always does with a tyrant that is so in control of how things are perceived. No, not a single drop of blood will be spilled. But, believe me, many eyes will be opened. Believe me! That's what I'm after. I will dedicate every fibre of my being to opening eyes and freeing minds. To have Indians first rebel against themselves, against their dependencies, so that they are of the right mind to rebel against their oppressors."

"Impossible!" yelled a passenger.

"Possible!" exclaimed Gurdit, and he took in a deep breath. "When men work together, anything is possible. Anything!"

"So how," the passenger continued, "do we do this? What do you propose we do?"

There was a short silence. Gurdit regarded us all. Then he simply said, "A fire..."

"A fire," repeated a passenger, and his eyes went wide with astonishment.

"The biggest fire you can possibly imagine," he said and crossed his arms and stared at us, smiling. We fell silent; we didn't know what to think. "We will march across the Punjab," he continued. He began to walk toward a cooking fire. "We will gather people from village to village, educating and informing them about the lesson that was ours to learn." He threaded his way around brass cooking pots. "We will ask them to follow us and to bring with them everything they own that is British." Passengers pushed against each other revealing a path to the fire for Gurdit. Gurdit held the newspaper up in the air and approached the fire. "And as we march across we will buy every single newspaper there is to buy. Once we have all the newspapers, we will end our march..." He threw the newspaper in the fire and turned to us. "...we will start a fire with those newspapers and in that fire everyone will throw what they have become dependant upon." He stopped, and our thoughts moved inward. I saw in my mind's eye a huge blaze; I saw you and your mother and our cousins and uncles and aunts, our entire village thrusting newspapers and jackets and forks and knives into its hungry flames. And then I saw British soldiers quitting our country, marching onto boats, and sailing back to England.

Gurdit left us to our imaginings. After a short time he continued, "And by doing this…by doing this we will have taken the first step toward liberation. By burning the newspapers we will have destroyed the tyrant's first tool of silent oppression." He paused to think about his words. He moved about the passengers. Sunny watched him with awe, nodding his head very slowly, deeply moved by the images in his mind. I turned to Amar; his expression was of a man who had heard the words and speeches countless times before, but had never seen anything real come of them. Amar shook his head gravely; he seemed to have stumbled over a thought that none of us had considered. I tore my eyes from him when Gurdit continued, "And it will not stop there. The newspapers will undoubtedly attempt to discredit us in an attempt to save face after our great fire. At this, we ourselves will use the power of the written word to free India!" Sunny's eyes lit up. Gurdit continued, "For I have thought about it long and hard and I now realize the only way to beat the tyrant is not with guns and bullets, which will merely be more fodder for the newspapers to use against us, but with handbills and posters, which will expand minds, inform, and educate. We will teach Indians to stop buying British goods, to sabotage their factories, and to turn in their guns and stop enslaving their own. This, my brothers, is how you beat the tyrant. If they cannot profit by being in our country, if they cannot control our opinions and our habits with their newspapers, they will leave! If they still refuse to leave, then, we will have no choice but to resort to violence."

He turned and walked toward his cabin. Then, as an afterthought, he faced us once more and said, "I don't expect all of you to follow me. I don't. I know how much you miss your families. But I know one thing: I would sacrifice a lifetime of joy just to make sure my family, my children, and my grandchildren, grow up in a country that is their own. I will follow the dictates of my soul. I suggest you all do the same." Gurdit grabbed his boy, placed him on his shoulders, and his boy shouted, "Waheguru Ji Ka Khalsa," and we answered in unison, "Waheguru Ji Ki Fateh!" Then Gurdit, carrying his boy, returned to their cabin and left us in meditative silence. And right there and then I could feel the men's hearts turning into one heart, the men's minds turning into one mind, and all of our worries, all of our anxieties, all of our personal problems melted away, replaced by a cause greater than ourselves.

July 22

The sun rose and talk of home and of the great fire was everywhere. As we watched the people fringing the shore and looking upon us with curiosity, Sunny, after a soft and most serious conversation with himself, said, "Would you teach my son how to read and write?" I looked at him, looked at the wooden horse in his hand, and said, "I will." Then he turned back to the water and said, "Thank you." And that was all he said to me all day.

At night we all huddled around Ali, watching him with unblinking eyes. We sat and talked and kept each other company and tried our best to make Ali smile. Many times he rewarded our efforts with a grin. As night progressed, a silence fell upon us, and we were soon talking about what we would do when we reached home. "You really think," Sunny began, "that a fire will make a difference?" "I'm not sure," I answered. "I think, maybe..." Amar interrupted, "I think he is a dreamer. I think he is crazy. And I think he is right and wrong at the same time. He is right that the first step toward liberation is freeing minds, but he is gravely mistaken if he thinks this will ever happen. But because he is crazy, because he is a dreamer, and because his heart is for his people, I will follow him to the very ends of this universe. That, I will do."

There was a momentary silence, then I said, "Could happen. I have never seen such a fire or such a protest..." Amar said, "Once long ago it could have worked. But now, though the people look the same,"-- he shook his head solemnly-- "they are not the same. A different kind of man walks the earth today. Less concerned about the welfare of others...much more concerned about the opinions of others." Amar thought about the fire, shook his head again, and continued, "No, it could never happen. Not anymore. So long as men's lives aren't affected by the tyrant's evil they won't lift a finger for another man. No, Gurdit has too much faith in the human heart. Yes, that's what it is. He believes so much in the heart that he has never once considered the prison of ego and fear that enslaves it." I considered his words and before I could add anything

105

he continued, "So long as they are being spoon-fed by the tyrant, men won't want to believe what we have to say."

"They will believe," said Sunny.

I remained silent.

Amar gazed into Sunny's eyes and said, "They will believe the newspapers before they will believe us. They will believe the newspapers because the newspapers will allow them to continue their lives without guilt, without the feeling that their lives collaborate in the enslavement of the world." He paused, shook his head, and sighed a deep and heavy sigh. "There are no more lions. The only lions I have ever known are right here with me on this ship. The rest, the men I served with, the men I died with, were nothing more than sheep. I was a sheep." He laughed sarcastically, pulled at his beard, and said, "A sheep in lion's clothing. Born a lion and all my life I baahed like a sheep. Only now, because of you, because of this ship, am I rediscovering what the tyrant had so cleverly stamped out of me." His eyes began to water and it was a while before the pain in his throat would allow him to continue. "I killed my own." He spoke slowly. It was a difficult confession. "I killed my own because I was a sheep. The men standing beside me let me kill my own because they were sheep..."

The anger was climbing in his throat and his voice crackled. He stopped. I gently put my hand on his shoulder. He looked down at it and then put his hand over mine. He heaved a deep breath, swallowed his anger, swallowed his regret, and vowed, "No more! No more the sheep! No more the sheep that sits in the tyrant's lap being spoon-fed and distracted with one hand while the other steals and starves my own." He sighed heavily. "These are clever tyrants and I am glad we will go after the newspapers, for it is only through them that the tyrant may create the prison of fear that enslaves the heart; and it is through them that they create the environment of fear and distraction they need to continue their abuses. It is only in this type of environment that they are able to transform fearless lions into poverty and death fearing sheep, for no tyrant can abuse the jungle when watchful lions are on the prowl. And every tyrant will do their best to turn lions into sheep. This is the way things are. This is the way things have to be, as sheep will forever be easier to control than lions." He paused, then continued. "One glimpse at any newspaper and the transformation begins. First the fear of opinion, then the fear of loss, then the fear of aging, then the fear of death...soon no more lion. Just a sheep in lion's clothing."

"We will spread the truth," Sunny asserted.

"It will amount to nothing," whispered Sanjay, never taking his eyes off Ali.

"No," said Sunny, "You're wrong. If out of the thousands we speak to, the truth frees but one mind, if one man is saved, then all our efforts were worth it."

Amar nodded in solemn agreement. He considered something carefully and deeply, and then he asked, "Do you actually believe that, with a war on the horizon, the King is going to take even the slightest chance of losing his greatest soldiers?" I turned to him and met his gaze, which was now deep and inward. "What do you mean?" I asked uneasily. Amar shook his head and sighed. "I'm not exactly sure," he said. Then he repeated softly, "I'm not exactly sure..." Ali looked up with a struggle. His pale eyes moved slowly from one worried face to the other. His lips moved and parted; they endeavoured to say something but failed in every attempt. Unable to speak words of comfort, he extended his hand out to us and one by one we took it and held it tightly until all five of us were holding the same hand.

July 23

Yesterday the trucks came thundering to the pier, one after the other, and their contents were transferred to a tug. The tug dragged itself to Nanak Jahaz whereupon oil and flour and lentils and barrels of water were hauled on board. With the help of local Indians and some immigration officers, everything was placed on board just before dawn. Once all was aboard the captain and his crewmen prepared the ship, and the ship groaned and whispered and belched black puffs of smoke into the air. Gurdit gathered us by the rail with his boy on his shoulders. The anchor rose loudly and, after a moment, Nanak Jahaz began its long voyage home.

As we pulled out into the ocean, Gurdit asked that we smile and wave politely to let the people of Vancouver know that we harboured no ill feelings toward them and that all would be taken care of in India. Amar stared at Hopkinson and Moustache. He said, "They will be given medals of honour for their crimes." And we stared at them and wished things had been different. We wished they hadn't treated us the way they had, and we felt sorry for them; for to treat people as they had treated us suggested minds imprisoned in dungeons of hate and intolerance.

The pier was crowded with onlookers who had not come to wish us a safe and pleasant trip, but who had come to continue what the actors had begun long ago. They sang loud and proud that their Canada should stay white forever, and we watched them with the deepest sympathy. Some of us smiled and waved good-bye; some of us just grinned; and some of us, despite Gurdit's words, took off our shoes and sandals and waved them angrily at Hopkinson. As we pulled out of the harbour, Sanjay came up behind us with Ali wrapped around his back. Sunny and I took Ali from Sanjay, each placing an arm around our necks to support him. We watched the battleship follow us and we watched the skiffs and the patrol boats circle around us. It almost seemed like a regatta. Then, all of a sudden, Gurdit's boy began to sing, and the song spread amongst us until we were enveloped by the words of our ancestors. Those words drowned out the shouts and cleansed our souls of the anger around us. I closed my eyes and lost myself in the hymn. When I opened my eyes, we were far out into the ocean, and the battleship and the patrol boat and the skiffs had all disappeared like a bad dream.

Soon the air turned fresh and chilly. The passengers sought refuge from the cold below deck. Slowly they melted away until only a few remained. Sunny and I stayed to watch the horizon. As the day progressed, Sunny began to mumble to himself. Then, staring at the sun slowly sinking behind the horizon, he said, "There are things greater than land." I nodded and said, "There are." He sighed, turned to me, then back to the horizon. "My son," he said, "will know how to read." He paused; then continued, "He will know how to read and he will know how to write. My son will know the books and he will know the laws. And with this knowledge he will help his people. He will help his people and he will not lose himself in ego as so many who read and write do. My son will fight and his weapon will be his words and his words will be whispered in every village. His words will grow in men's hearts like a divine rose and his words will open eyes and free minds and wherever there is abuse in the world his words will come alive in men, and those men will not turn their backs on the oppressed, but will help the oppressed no matter what their skin colour or nationality. His words will build a fortress against fear and intolerance and his words will remind men that we all share the same soul, that another man's suffering is his own suffering." I placed my hand on his shoulder and said, "I will teach your son...I will teach your son and he will do these things." He turned to me and nodded. He then turned to the sunset and said, "I know you will."

July 24

Under a cover of darkness, I spent the whole night watching the stars shimmer in the sea. I watched the water as I thought about home, you, your mother, and the lessons. There is a lesson in everything: a smile, a look, a glance, a song, a gesture, and, always, a journey. And in this journey there is more than the bitter lesson of our true status within the Empire. There is the divine lesson of perseverance and selflessness, of love and friendship, of cooperating and pulling through, of making the best of any and every situation; whether bitter or sweet, happy or sad, difficult or easy. There is the lesson of men imprisoned in ego and the brothers they would betray for that ego. And then there is the golden lesson of strangers: the kindness and generosity of large-hearted men who we had never known and who we will never know. My son, I can still see that man on his crutches hobbling through the crowd, slowly making his way to the collection table to sacrifice all his savings to lessen our suffering. That image is burned in my mind and I take it with me wherever I go. I take it with me like a treasure--a treasure I wouldn't trade for all the gold in the world.

But of all the lessons, the crowning lesson of all this is a lesson in character. Throughout this ordeal, no matter what these men have done to us, we have not changed for the worse. We have not, in bitterness, assimilated their anger or hate and, regardless of the pain and mental torment they have subjected us to, we will continue to respect their humanity. And this, my son, is not an obvious or implied lesson, for more often than not, when a man is abused for long enough he often loses exactly what his abusers sought to destroy. And more often than not, he puts on the mask of his abuser and continues the abuse. No man has the right to abuse another, even if that man has been abused. This, my son, my beautiful son, is the lesson.

Now, when I reflect on the ship and its passengers, I fail to see them as separate entities. When I think of our journey, I think about how the ship and the passengers and the crewmen became one. So if ever you think or talk or tell the story of the Komagata Maru, you are not thinking or talking or telling the story of a rickety old rusted steamship carrying a few hundred farmers across the Pacific to start a new life for their families, but of Nanak Jahaz, a living, breathing being whose blood was men, whose mission was noble, whose struggle was harsh, but whose lesson was divine. No, my son, when one day you tell the story of Nanak Jahaz you will not be talking about units, items, elements, and individuals, but about one entity, one spirit, one soul, and about how your father was more than proud to be part of such an entity, such a spirit, such a soul. Now, as one, we will do what must be done. We will take the first step toward our freedom and independence. And when this is done, I will return home and hold both you and your mother and never let go! I love you my son. I will be back soon. I promise.

Epilogue

There was more to read but the sergeant had read enough. He closed the journal gently and held it to his heart. He stared at the man before him and tasted copper in his mouth. Reading the journal he had unknowingly bit into his cheek, and now the blood mixed with his saliva and slithered down his throat. He lifted his gaze to his superiors, ground his teeth, and saw them with new eyes. They kicked and poked and prodded the bodies with the indifference of a butcher testing meat. The sergeant closed his eyes, took in a deep breath, and knew he was no longer the same man. At the sound of laughter he opened his eyes. He looked at his rifle and then at the lifeless man before him. The tears began. He could feel something stirring within him, something greater than himself. He released his rifle and it splashed in the dark pool. He rose slowly and unsteadily, without taking his eyes off the man. He turned to the troops and to his superiors and watched three of them struggle to pry something out of a corpse's hand. When finally they succeeded, they examined the object in the fading moonlight. The sergeant made out the silhouette of a horse. His superiors laughed at the toy with intense amusement and soon lobbed it over the railway tracks. They then stepped over the body and moved along with the same cold indifference. The sergeant swallowed a breath, turned his back on his superiors, and took a step forward. It was the first step of a great and meaningful journey. But that, readers and listeners, is another story.

Gratitude

No book was ever written alone. From first draft to final draft a book is the accomplishment of the author as well as the friends and family who encouraged, supported, and motivated him. That said, I would like to express my infinite gratitude to Waheguru for having placed this story on my path, for having instilled within me the courage to act, and for having blessed me with the guidance, assistance, and encouragement of so many kind and talented people. I owe these people my deepest and most heartfelt gratitude.

To the indomitable strength and determination of my grandparents and parents whose sweat, hard work, and sacrifice afforded me the luck and opportunity to write.

This book could have never been written without the love and support of my sister and brothers. I thank them for their endless encouragement, unconditional love, and for always believing I was capable of the impossible.

I will never be able to thank my darling Regina--My Lady Beautiful--and the five brothers of my heart-- Dave, Xavier, Ken, Mark, and Kabir--for their strength and friendship, for their time and generosity, and for believing my book into being.

A warm hug and many thanks to all my uncles, aunties, and cousins: Genevieve, Alexandre, Oliver, Simon, Matthieu, Michael Anthony, Mon Oncle Guy, Mon Oncle Denis, Mon Oncle Ernest, Ma Tante Johanne, Ma Tante Lucie, Ma Tante Luce, Raj, Kiran, Charren, Simrin, Amrit, Sanj, Dave, Ranjit, Sonia, Nav, Nageena, Rup, Rik, Amar, Pavan, Sandeep, Amrita, Bernard, Anthony-Michael, Natasha, Nicola, Naveena, Mark, Alex, Larissa, Sandy, Manjinder, Amrita, Alexander, Prete, Didar, Amar, Amrit, Depee, Robert, Tanya, Robert, Torben, John, Teji Uncle, Pinde Uncle, Hinde Uncle, Bepe Uncle, Pami Uncle, Ursula Auntie, Lilian Auntie, Gurinder Auntie, Rani Auntie, Prem Auntie, Pritpal Auntie.

Another hug to my dear friends: Janet, a brilliant editor and teacher; Jnr, a magnificent director and filmmaker; Carlos, a friend I could always count on; Vageli, a poem in the ring (keep on smiling!); Nick, my best buddy since elementary; George and his family who were a great part of my teen life and who enriched those years with the grace and mirth of Greek culture and hospitality.

And yet another hearty hug to all the members of the Sardinian folk-dancing team for making the World Festival of Island Cultures an unforgettable and most divine experience: Saddi Antonio, Mammarella Aldo, Pilia Diego, Cirina Fabrizio, Marras Matteo, Dessi Pino, Mereu Antonio, Mereu Sauro, Puddu Mario, Piras Cenzo, Lecis Lazzaro, Pani Andrea, Cubeddu Massimiliano, Benevento Alessia, Murtas Alice, Murtas Simona, Russo Stefania, Vincis Raffaele, Mereu Faustino, Atzori Dario, Pani Annarita, Caria Maurizio.

To the amazing family in Rio de Janeiro who shared their lives with me and who showed me all that was beautiful in their country: Filipe, Tia Maria, Tia Regina, Daniele, Tio Toni, Renato, Tatiana, Duda, Andreas, Marcelo, Bianca, and Gustav.

To Kids College, Class#5, and all the wonderful friends I made in Seoul: Sheldon and Ian, for giving me a second chance; Wayne and John for their inspirational and most riveting conversations by the coffee machine; Kirk, for his witty opinions and observations; Donald, for his insights; Lise, for her wonderful humour; Toska, for her help in a time of need; Casey and Karenna, for being wonderful dance partners; Evan, for just being a good friend; Coreana, for a dinner never forgotten; Greg, for taking me on a tour of his studio and introducing me to the wonderful world of animation; Korea, for being one of my great teachers.

Thanks to Stephanie and Martha for looking over my work. Thanks to Gigi and Sukhi for their hospitality. Thanks to the brilliant and talented friends who shared time with me in Surrey: Raj, Nick, Paul, and Amarjit. I would also like to thank the kind and most helpful woman who helped me better understand the dreams, experiences, and motivations of the passengers aboard the Komagata Maru. Your anonymity remains safe with me; just know that this book could have never been written without your vital input. I would also like to acknowledge the historical and exhaustive research done by Sohan Singh Josh, whose book--Tragedy of the Komagata Maru --served as a guiding light.

A special note of gratitude to the province of British Columbia for taking so much pride in their library, and to the staff of the Vancouver Public Library for being so pleasant, efficient, and resourceful. (If you haven't been to Vancouver, the library alone is worth the visit!) And finally, a humble bow to Grand Master Chong Lee for bringing Tae Kwon Do to Quebec, and to Darrell Henegan for taking all the confused and negative energy of a misunderstood youth and directing it in a more positive direction.

Jessi Thind is a private Tae Kwon Do instructor in Montreal and a freelance script consultant for a film and game consulting firm that helps writers, game designers, and studio executives evaluate and shape their ideas. This is his first novel.

ISBN 141201301-1